THE
ADVENTURE POEM
OF
JULIUS CINNAMON

Spiral Machines

First published in 2017 by

Spiral Machines

409-2881 Richmond Road
Ottawa, ON
K2B-8J5

ISBN-13: 978-1-7750835-0-4

www.pattmayne.com
www.spiralmachines.ca

THE
ADVENTURE POEM
OF
JULIUS CINNAMON

Chapter 1

The cold water is a smash in the face. Indeed, the frigid splash envelopes my entire body as I plummet naked into the ocean from the helicopter which is now fludding away. *Flud flud flud* it says as I sink into the icy depths of a salty frothing winter embrace. The sweet liquid allows me to penetrate it and then it penetrates me with its brisk temperature. All my senses are deliciously alive and I am surrounded, tingling with the brutality of the medium into which I have been delivered.

Swim, fucker, swim! Kicking and digging upwards I reach for the shimmering sky until finally my beard explodes a spray of ocean into the noisy air. Well, not that noisy, but there's a special openness of sound when you're suddenly not submerged. But no time to relish the taste of oxygen. Head for the dock! *Stroke stroke stroke!* The strength of my body brings me joy as I propel myself through the waves which seek to pull me under. I grab the ladder and *one, two, three,* I'm up! Standing naked and dripping before Felix and Victor, hands on hips, water streaming from my cock onto the boards of the dock.

Felix with his broad jaw, a prosthetic replacement grown from his own stem-cells, his scars visible lines of jagged lightning where the beard won't grow after the surgery. He looks damn good in that suit and his hair slicked back like it's a hundred years ago. He clutches a bottle of fine vodka. Victor regards me with his one eye, the other a black electronic gadget reading God-knows-what information and pumping it directly into his brain. He clutches his cane, of course, rubbing his thumb over the top like he wants to flick it open and press whatever buttons lay beneath.

My two Frankenstein monsters, old friends and easy enemies, sitting in lush velvet easy chairs on the windy dock, are not impressed by my helicopter ice-dive entrance or the terms on which I agreed to meet them. But Felix still leans forward and pours a shot into each of the three glasses sitting on the battered wooden table and we all swallow a mouthful of fine alcohol, peppery and smooth. It burns as it goes down, a welcome contrast to my thrillingly freezing exterior. The grin on my face is a snarl of perpetual challenge and triumph. I wave them toward the sauna which I ordered built just for this meeting. The city of New York beneath a layer of snow lays sprawled out beyond the dock but we don't care about that.

"Come, my Russian patriarchs," I say, my throat ripping the wind. "We have things to discuss."

My stern bodyguards wait inside, broad-shouldered and dressed in suits not quite as expensive as those of Felix and Victor. They offer me a towel and help my guests remove their clothes as a wizened Native American pours tea over the hot coals in the centre of the wooden cavern.

My employees leave us wearing nought but towels and sweat. The warm air requires effort to inhale, thick like smoke as I perceive my companions across the misty chamber. The hairy expanse of Felix's muscular chest is juxtaposed against the folded layers of old skin drooping off Victor's shoulders. Yet they both regard me with keen interest, waiting for me to speak first. And so I grin and do not speak, for it was they who requested this meeting and me who has all the answers. Information is always a commodity, and now more than ever!

Felix, less proud and more commanding, is the first to cave. "This land in the Congo. It is not your usual affair. I was not aware you even had the means to exploit such resources!"

Victor chimes in, rapping his cane impatiently on the wooden floor to express the energy of his interest in the matter. "It is very suspicious," he says with his much thicker Russian accent, "that nobody knows what you will do there, and nobody is a part of your plan. We work together in many ventures, you and I. Is my experience with real estate no longer of interest to you?"

I peer at them, not so much studying as simply enjoying the discomfort that they feel in their ignorance. Indeed, Felix operates many mines in Africa and must naturally be curious about my mysterious venture. And Victor and I have made hordes of money together through our various connections and collaborations in land deals. It is unsurprising that they are surprised, yet oddly presumptuous for them to take such a personal interest in a private business adventure.

My narrow-eyed expression explodes into a happy and welcoming smile as I hold wide my muscular arms in a gesture of embrace. "Comrades," I boom merrily, "there was no plan to cut you out of any deal. I'm simply involved in an experiment which promises no guaranteed financial rewards. Profits should be shared among collaborators, but what about the losses from foolhardy excursions? Should I drag you into the pit with me? Rest assured, you have no interest in this project."

They are not convinced. From the shining stone of Felix's steady eyes one might imagine he was a mere layer of skin pulled over a statue where only the optical cavities displayed the true material of the man, like his skin is protecting us from viewing the unbearable power beneath. Victor writhes like a dying snake, snarling and shaking. "Then you will not mind sharing with us what this project is," the old man spits.

"I do indeed mind," I tell him gravely, no longer playing nice. "We're familiar enough to speak plainly, old friends, and this is a private venture. We all have our little projects and schemes, and I don't ask for explanations when you buy old hotels which never open to the public, or your private firms purchase chemicals and equipment but never sell anything on the open market. That's right, I know about these things! And I'm proud of my friends who have their fingers in many pies! Yet here you are, openly scrutinizing my own plans. You make me sad."

Felix could almost be my younger brother. Our builds, beards, and hunters' eyes are not quite identical, but certainly variations on a theme. "It is unusual that you would embark on mining alone, when you know my equipment goes unused in a nearby dig. Surely you could save money and time by including me in your plans."

"And you know who my friends are, and what they owe me," Victor added. "I could get you that land for a fraction of the cost!"

Now I must calculate to which extent I will appease my guests and their emotions, and how much I will disregard their intrusion and blast onto the next stage of my plan. I had not anticipated such emotion and interest, but I find that I am more pleased than concerned. If only they knew the extent of my ambitions! But the details are ridiculous and the scheme is not yet complete, and I cannot indulge their curiosity or my vanity by painting a picture of the goings-on near the volcanic mines that I've purchased. Can they deduce that my intentions are not as simple as merely mining the metals for resale on the market? Of course I would have included them in such an endeavour. It is for that kind of plan that I have allies in business. The fact that I have not engaged their assistance should be proof that the mere mining of metals is not my main mark.

"Express to me a precise request," I say, "So I can offer a concise response."

"Include us in your plan," Felix says plainly enough. "We are curious and greedy, just like you."

"I appreciate your candour and constant collaboration," I say truthfully, almost choking up. "But you have nothing to offer, and nothing to gain."

"Then simply tell us!" Victor demands, clanking his cane again on the floor.

I slowly shake my head and stand. "The success of this project depends on redundant discretion," I explain. "Consider it an art project, and me a neurotic creator who cannot stand for his creation to see the light of day until it's ready. Now I must leave. I'm sorry for bringing you here without satisfying your curiosity or your greed, but I have met you as you asked, and you have my response."

As I turn to leave, Victor says, "We will discover your secret, mister Blackburn!" And he spits in the coals where his loogie hisses like a snake.

At the mention of that name my eyes snap with curiosity to the rude guest, but Felix is standing now with one hand on Victor's shoulder. The larger man locks me with his gaze and says, "Forgive our senile old friend, who forgets names from time to time. We wish you luck on your plan, whatever it may be, my dear Julius Maxwell Cinnamon."

I grip the strong man's hand, but the message has been delivered that they can find my secrets as easily as I have found theirs. Is Felix genuinely apologetic when he reaffirms my identity with my full name? Or is he merely playing good cop in this shrewd negotiation? "If only we were more rivals and less friends," I say as I pump the hearty claw. "What a fun game that would be."

My submarine is waiting and there are many details which need my attention. I bid my friends farewell and throw aside my towel, emerging naked once more into the crisp winter air to behold the metal capsule which has risen from the depths to whisk me away. Across the plank I go and down into the moderate warmth of the vessel where my captain greets me with fresh clothes and a hot meal. He knows where I must go and I retire to my cabin to read as he takes me there.

Chapter 2

Our man-made infrastructure of buildings and vehicles creates a wall to protect us from nature, enclosing us with all that is healthy and supreme for our fine-tuned bodies, our consciousness machines. We clamp ourselves into these sanctums not to escape the annoying horrors of nature, but to explore them! "Freeze me, will you?" we dare Father Winter. Our igloos and houses defy him. When the vacuum of space threatens to explode our lungs we capture the air in a canister and stomp on the moon. "Would you like to drown me?" I ask the ocean, teasing it, dangling human sacrifice like a bright carrot. Down into its depths I go in my submarine, piloted by an expert who feasts upon my payroll. I wish all were well fed enough to explode their potential upon the Earth, from schizophrenic alcoholic to disciplined neurosurgeon, don't let those brain cells wither. But I can only direct my funds at those who are within my scope, and so my happy captain is enriched with vitamins and pride as we part the seas on a sub-nautical route toward my destination.

My cabin is like a prison cell. Rugged toilet, hard thin bed, picture of my daughter's comically stern face bolted to the concave metal wall. The picture is outdated, from when she was a teenager. Unlike a prison cell I have a desk of oak, and in the bottom drawer some scotch. I sit in a chair and read *Post Scarcity Anarchism* for the sixth time, searching more for flaws instead of ideas now. Such rare silence down here, barely the rumble or hum of machinery, so faint that I have to strain to hear and even then it must be my imagination. If I had even the slightest hint of tinnitus it would drown out the sub and I would believe myself to be in silence. When one day I write my memoirs I think I will hire this same captain to take me into the deep solitude of this lonely liquid joy, so every page will be pressurized with meaning and no worldly pleasures or dangers shall intrude. But will it be the depths of this Earthly ocean? I want a spaceship that doubles as a submarine, made of glass so my eyes can devour every environment.

Finally we ascend. I know because the pilot

communicates via electronic gadgetry, but also from the lone creak that echoes across the hull as it adjusts to a lesser level of pressure. I love that danger-sound of wrenching metal and my pupils dilate as Poseidon himself seems to speak through the rising pitch of the monosyllable question, "Would you like a watery death?" *Creeeaaak.*

I comb my beard and hair and put on a fine suit. Charcoal grey, blue shirt, the slightest glint of gold-gilt and watch-strap. What a handsome man! I don't think I would trade any degree of my handsomeness or ruggedness, in either direction, for the balance is so perfectly complete. If only I had a scar to mitigate my vanity.

I leave the book behind so the surface-folks on the train won't get the wrong impression (or rather, the correct impression). Though nobody knows who I am, I still have an image to project. I'll get a newspaper or magazine which befits my role. My only burden is a small leather suitcase holding pyjamas and toiletries. I climb up the ladder like a Ninja Turtle, and swing open the hatch to let in the cold rush of winter air. My man is already waiting for me as I climb out of the tube and onto the deck of the sub.

"Armand," I say as the African's strong black hand clasps my own. He helps me into the little deck boat, the sun shining like an aura behind his unnecessary navy-captain's cap. Also unnecessary are the AK 47 and hunting knife he carries, and I know he has throwing knives in a khaki vest beneath the thick jacket, lined with fur. The marijuana I smell on him is perhaps necessary, considering the torments that plagued his life before I hired him. Even such a strong man as Armand Urbain would be haunted by those memories, but instead he smiles, always smiles, and never lets me down.

"New neighbours, mister Cinnamon," my Congolese henchman informs me as he steers the boat toward my dock at the marina. He points with one long arm.

Indeed I had noticed the new boats, mid-sized yachts on the dock across from my own. "Are you sure the old neighbours didn't just get new boats?"

"I see the ledger, mister Cinnamon," Armand confirms. "New neighbours. Their name is Jones."

"Since when?"

"Two days ago. I have not seen them yet."

Now he is tying up the boat and I step onto the thick wooden planks of the dock. My own humble sailing boat rests near the end, beyond this small deck boat. Those new yachts seem to put my meagre fleet to shame, but my submarines and cargo vessels are elsewhere putting plans into motion, hidden from the eyes of my swank marine-mates. I peer up and down the docks, curious as to the persons who could afford such sea-crafts, and why they chose this dock beside mine instead of one of the many empty slots. And so soon after it was vacated? Mid-winter seems an odd time to bring your boats to a new marina, though there could certainly be a legitimate reason for that.

"Any news?" I ask my man.

"Good news," he tells me, and delivers an envelope. "I had to offer more money, but they will deliver the goods. Details inside, my friend. They have chosen a price and a location, but they are yet to choose a time. They will call me, and I will pass it on to you."

My anxiousness has turned to gold just as the sun kisses the horizon of houses up from the shore. I put the envelope in my jacket for later study. "Do you trust them?"

Armand shakes his head. "I trust no-one but you, Mr. Cinnamon, and the goddess Marijuana, and the weapon in my hand. But you know we will have that technology, one way or the other. If they do not follow through, it is they who will suffer."

A taxi arrives at the end of the wharf and honks its horn. "You have my ticket?" I ask, and Armand hands me a train ticket. "The engineers are expecting you in a few days," I remind him.

"It is all in order."

"I'll see you when we buy the goods."

"Let's hope you don't have to!"

I head toward my ride, putting on sunglasses

to protect me from the permanent explosion in space, burning and burning. Armand behind me says, "Glorious day! Soon we will have a new home."

"Train station," I tell the cab driver, and off we go. Soon the sun is flitting between the suburban houses. The fat driver plays soft Mexican music, and the cab smells like chicken McNuggets. We pass under a concrete bridge which separates these suburbs from downtown, and I anticipate my arrival at the train depot.

What has never left my mind are those two new yachts. My new neighbours who so quickly replaced the old. There is, of course, no need for concern. I use a false name to rent my space at the marina and none of my rivals know my erratic travels habits. Alas, my paranoia seeks an adventure I can never have. If only I were so careless that somebody could rend my plans asunder, forcing me into a struggle to put it all back together. A careless thought! The imminent project is vastly more interesting.

Yet I cannot suppress a satisfied grin when I receive Armand's text message, just as we arrive at the busy train station. "The Jones' are on their way." My reply is that I look forward to meeting them. "Mr. Jones is wearing that red jacket you bought him, but has died his hair that awful blonde again," Armand adds, unnecessarily innocuous.

"His brother still has the creepy brown trenchcoat." He knows I have never met them, let alone purchased their coats. Now I know who to look for. Hilariously, my work is done for the week and I am heading home to my mountain estate in the Canadian Rockies. There is nothing left for them to spy on, since my address is no secret. But now I can spy on them! That is, if they make it in time to catch this train. But how will they know which train I'm taking? Several are ready for departure. I'll make it easy for them. I have time, so I head to the shop inside the station and buy a cigar, a newspaper, and some magazines. With my reading material under my arm and my small suitcase by my feet, I wait outside the train and observe the traffic as more passengers arrive.

I speculate about who my pursuers may be. We'll assume that Jones is a false name. Armand says they rented the space at the marina two days ago, which was roughly when Felix and Victor finally convinced me to meet them today to discuss my private plans, when I dictated my unreasonable conditions for the meeting. It seems most obvious that they hired these false Jones to follow me, and if that's the case I believe I have little to fear. We have made money together in the past, and as far as they are concerned we may make money again in the future. This tailgater could be the result of a totally natural curiosity. Perhaps I can have some fun with my spies, feed them false information somehow, or just toy with their emotions.

But there are other candidates, other suspects in this crime. Like my contact from the university. Soon I will be purchasing rare and expensive technology, absolutely vital for my ambitious project. Armand negotiated the deal because he's more familiar with the criminal underworld, a more imposing character. Naturally they have cast their net for information about the buyer, but how did they learn who I am? How did they discover the dock? Maybe they followed Armand and not me at all, but that doesn't explain how they rented the space at the marina two days ago, before they knew Armand's name. No. Either this traitorous employee of The Technical University of Sunderwich has access to otherworldly information gathering techniques, or my pursuers hail from a different flock.

And here they are. A late model sedan ejects a man with perfect blonde hair and a red sports jacket. I'm almost jealous of that hair, as my own perfect black hair just can't achieve the same visual depth as lighter colours, and I don't think a man should dye his mane. Some day soon I will naturally develop grey streaks, but for now the nondescript noir is the price I pay for my ripe virility.

Nobody else exits the car, which drives away. I can't see Mr. Jones' eyes behind his highway-cop shades. He lights a cigarette and takes a look around, adjusts his jacket. The trainyard is archways of brick, cement, and of course trains. All I can smell is winter, oil, and my cigar. My spy contrasts so sharply against the ageing urban architecture that he is a magazine ad. It is probably even an expensive cigarette. I want to give him a glass of cognac, and push him in front of a train. Eye contact? Yes please. I keep mine locked on him, waiting for him to notice me. He must have spotted me long ago, because I'm the only thing he doesn't look at. He's really nursing that cigarette.

The train man asks to look at my ticket. I show him the long string of first-class stubs. "All the way to British Columbia!" I announce loud enough for a handsome man to hear me from across the platform. The train man gives me a condescending smile that says, *good for you!* Assured that I can't make my presence and destination any more obvious, I snub the cigar in a nearby ashtray and head into the train to begin my two day trip, mobile vacation with this unexpected companion. I disappear into my cabin, kick off my shoes, and sleep before the train leaves the station.

I awake with the dawn, refreshed, and look out my little window at the leafless branches whipping past in front of the sun. I love to ride the train. An airplane would get me home by morning, by transforming me into cattle. I prefer the scenic route, locked in a private cabin with some reading material and my thoughts. They have a whole car just for eating and drinking. I once bought some land from a man I met on a train, developed that land into cabins for tourists, and sold it for twice what it was worth. More than once I've engaged in a sexual affair with a woman I met at the mobile bar. Our relationships began and ended in a high-speed tube of metal. I'm always on the lookout for these adventures, and it seems that this time a new kind of adventure has followed me into my safe haven. Good, I say.

I loathe to brush my teeth before breakfast, but at least my toothpaste has no minty flavour. My feast awaits two cars down, and I offer a clean smile to the few early-risers who I pass on the way. None of them are my blonde shadow. I order a salad, sausage, and coffee from the round faux-wood bar, and sit at a booth to enjoy my repast with a finance magazine I've brought. The light comes almost horizontally through the windows in that special way that happens in the morning, and I feel a camaraderie with the three other people who are quietly talking and eating nearby. We are morning people, we are witnessing the dawn like a birth, like a prayer to the pagan wilderness.

My meal is gone and I've read three articles before Mr. Jones arrives for his own breakfast. He has left behind his jacket but not those sunglasses. Granted, the slant of the sun justifies them. I note his strong pecs beneath the blue t-shirt. With those strong arms, his build is almost identical to mine. I wonder which martial art he prefers. How is his ground game? I consider simply asking him. It's almost adorable, the way he pretends to ignore me on his way to order his food.

We could play that silent game. What if I stole his wallet? How many of his secrets would easily be unveiled? Possibly his real name, but it wouldn't necessarily lead me to his employer, which is what I ultimately want to learn.

He orders a heartier breakfast with eggs, sausage, and potatoes. Now he has more carbs, and is ready for a fight. I order more coffee, and sit across from him.

"Good morning, mister Jones," I say.

He pushes down his shades to peer at me over the lenses. "You talking to me?"

He has removed his wallet from his back pocket, and placed it on the table. So I take it and remove his identification.

"The fuck are you doing?"

Beneath his picture is the name Rusty Knight. "I thought Rusty was always a nickname," I muse.

Rusty makes no attempt to regain his possessions, and shows no signs of distress. "Tell my parents that."

"Who do you work for?" I ask bluntly.

"I'm getting some cognitive dissonance here," Rusty says. "You dress like a millionaire, but you're acting like a homeless drunk."

I proceed to empty out his wallet, and find nothing interesting. Credit cards, some cash, various business cards. He hardly pays attention, just continues to eat. He's taken his self-mastery a little too far. If he was innocent as he pretended, wouldn't he have tried to stop me by now?

I study the business cards. A software company from Israel. A Jiujitsu training club in Seattle. A Spanish underwater-salvage company. Something in Mandarin with a picture of a horse-shoe magnet. Nothing links him to anybody I know. Still, I keep the business cards and leave the rest on the table.

He points at my jacket where I've stashed the cards. "I'm a good sport, okay? But those are my cards and I'm gonna need them back."

I'm reminded of stories of false accusations, where the mortified main character realizes he's been harassing the wrong person. And yet I persist. "Who hired you?"

"I'm not such a good sport that I'm gonna sit

here and answer your questions."

"That's alright," I tell him with a grin. "It's a two day ride. We've got lots of time to get to know each other."

I stand up, but he grabs my arm. I was prepared for that, and with my other hand I deftly squeeze near the artery in his wrist, genuinely seeking to maim him as quietly as possible. But he lets go, preferring not to cause a scene, and lets me walk away. Nobody seems to have noticed, and I take my magazine and new clues back to my cabin again. Locked away, I use my phone to visit the website for each business on those cards. There must be some connection to somebody I know, but among the listed staff or associated businesses nothing triggers my memory. Who is this man?

I Google his name and find his LinkedIn profile. It says he's in sales, and his clients include the ones from the business card, among others. For a moment I wonder if this is a trap, will they glean vital information from me after luring me onto their sites? But my phone is a throwaway and they must already know my name. I'm using the train's wifi. Again I wonder if I'm mistaken, and maybe I've just robbed an innocent man. But his generic "sales" title, and the various bits of bland motivational wisdom that pepper his portfolio, makes me think this is a digital false front.

This puzzle is frustrating, and that frustration

awakens my internal hunter. I need to discover who hired Rusty Knight. I'm tempted to call the businesses directly, using the phone numbers on the cards. But I'm wary of that slight chance that Rusty's whole persona is surrounded by an aura of false lures constructed to collect my data when I research him. So I delegate the work to Armand. With my phone I snap a photo of several of the cards, writing the name Rusty Knight on one with black ink. I send the photo in a text message which says, "Research." Armand responds right away with a confirmation that he will indeed pursue the trail.

This rented private cabin is much more comfortable than the one I keep in the sub, though I would trade this comfort for that portrait of my darling daughter. The one in my wallet is too small, and even more out of date. I recline now with the newspaper and absorb myself in the events of the previous day. War and violence, politicians talking, and the maneuverings of major corporations. Predictable categories of human drama. How rarely does one event break the mold and set the stage for the next epoch of our species' history? How long do these events brew unseen behind the veil before their symptoms bubble up and foretell the now-unavoidable transmutation? There is violent news in Africa today, but it does not seem to effect my project. But if something did throw a wrench in those gears, the newspaper is not how I would find out.

My phone vibrates lightly, politely. I assume it must be Armand with some news about Rusty Knight-Jones, but my assumption proves premature. It is Alex White, the man whose security team protects my African investment from locals and rivals. "Antivirus caught a bug in Agartha. Unknown source. Delete?"

We're using a simple code. A bug is any spy or invader who's trying to infiltrate my compound. The antivirus, as you may have guessed, is Alex's security team. Agartha is no codeword, it's the official title for the location of my unofficial project. I think we all know what "delete" means.

My reply: "Negative. Email virus to Olympus."

Olympus is another codeword, indicating my mountain home, which is where I'm heading. Of course this virus will not actually be emailed, but shipped very uncomfortably via airplane and helicopter and probably arrive before I do.

I take another look at those business cards. I'm infiltrated on two fronts. There has been no trouble until now. Hiccups, annoyances, and obstacles abound, as always, but before today my project has been free from schemes and attacks. This dual-front assault, this pincer-move, seems like an act of war. Are Victor and Felix so aggressive that they'll follow me and send their spy into a dangerous deep-African location? I've never known them to engage in such cloak-and-daggery. But who else could it be? Now I really want to interrogate Rusty Knight. I wonder if I can get him off this train, where nobody will see my rigorous methods. But I will probably have to let him go, and save my curiosity for the package en route to my private property.

Let him go? Well maybe not quite. Plenty of time yet to study, question, and annoy while on route. He's unlikely to call on the attention of the authorities, considering there's a clandestine aspect to his own adventure. But even though he knows that I know that he's following me, his cover may be secure enough to call the cops were I to, say, beat the shit out of him in my pursuit of the truth.

More text messages give me the dirt I need to form a clearer plan. Armand says, "Rusty Knight AKA Werner Holmes AKA Trent Levine murderer mercenary unknown employer."

"Good stuff. Thank you," I reply. A nervous reaction tells me to act now, to spend my energy. I can feel the squeeze from these unexpected intrusions into my affairs, and the unknown elements bug me, urge me to react. What if there are other spies who I haven't noticed? What if these are decoys? Now the train feels like a prison.

This is when I would go for a long run or a hearty swim to focus my mind and my physical energy. So much for a relaxing train ride. As always, a few deep breaths transform my frustrated energy to expansive good cheer.

When in doubt, meditate. I find the lotus position and focus on the rumble of the wheels as they roll metal over metal across this beautiful countryside. It hardly takes a minute for my instinctive silent mind to recognize the futility of frustration. Do I have problems? Not a single one. An enemy hides, and he has expressed himself in the form of two clumsy interlopers. They are opportunities to discover vital information. I mistook my excitement for fear. I want to dig into these men and unearth their secrets. But that excitement too could be a weakness, if I let it guide me. My only friend is every moment, and with these successive best friends I can carry all emotion forward with me. This is the essence of glory.

I read a few more articles from my magazine, then I decide it must be time for lunch. I leave behind my jacket and any jewelry that might get in the way during a scrimmage. My club sandwich and rum is exquisite. The countryside is a close-knit latticework of medium-sized trees. The trunks and branches appear extra dark against the light dusting of snow. I can barely see a broad river a couple hundred meters away, running parallel to our course, visible through the branches. The spots of blue are like diamonds that sparkle only for me. Hello, they seem to say, you champion of diamonds. I think I can die happy.

My plan is simple, and the first stage is the simplest of all. I will read until Rusty shows himself, and then I will ignore him. When he finally returns to his room, I will follow him. He needs to eat sometime. But as they day wanes I fill my mind with news until I can't read straight, stare out the window as the sun leans toward the other side, and still my friend has not come out to play. Can I sweet-talk the staff into telling me his cabin number? I can't imagine any method that would not arouse suspicion. Where is he? Hidden like his masters.

Another meal and a cup of coffee are necessary. Lighter this time with a chicken Caesar salad. While I order the food I'm rewarded with a new clue. Is it luck or is it vigilance? The bar-man is speaking on a phone, writing down an order on yellow paper. I only catch the tail end. "Bloody steak. Absolutely. We'll bring it to you when it's ready, Mr. Knight. Cabin fourteen. You're welcome."

As I consume another nutritious meal my paranoia rises up again. It certainly is convenient that the bartender received and conveyed that perfect bite of information just as I was ordering my own food. I look around at the other patrons, wondering if there is another spook among them, sending their own text messages to Rusty. When I knock on the door to cabin fourteen, when I enter, will there be three men waiting to ambush me? On the surface it seems that Mr. Knight doesn't want to face me, since his cover is blown and he can't casually observe me anymore. But maybe his plans are as violent as mine, and he means to beat my secrets out of me. Well good luck, Mr. Knight.

I finish my salad. They have already brought him his meal, and by now he will be part way through. I want to ambush him while his stomach is heavy with meat. I couldn't see what was beneath the metal lid of the plate they carried out of the restaurant car, but surely his bloody steak is accompanied by some kind of potatoes. He will be sluggish and slow, and I will be dynamite.

The time has come. The thick fabric napkin, baby blue, goes in my pocket. I pass by calmer people, relaxing in their seats. So many are reading or listening to music on their phones. Looking out the windows, having quiet conversations. A teenage couple are cuddling, whispering. But I am hunting. Past the general seating and into the first class cabin car. My unit is thirty-seven in the next car. Rusty is number fourteen, close at-hand. A bellboy nods at me as I pass him and I give him a hearty smile. Napkin wrapped tight around my left fist, I turn the latch on unit fourteen. It is blissfully, suspiciously unlocked and I casually step into my enemy's domain.

What can I expect? The first thing I hear is the clatter of fork and knife being placed onto a table. He's not expecting me, but he'll move fast. As I lock the door behind me, I dodge a flying fist which slams into the wall. I put both my hands on his chest and push him hard across the small space, so Rusty Knight stumbles and falls against the little table at the far end of his cabin. Now he's got a fork in his hand, already covered in cow's blood. My fists are up. We both know what I want. I want to pin the fucker down and beat answers out of him. What does he want? Whatever his original plans were, now he just wants to stab the problem away with that fork, and deal with the repercussions later.

At first he was nervous, but now he's settled into a ready stance, crouching a little, even grinning at me. "Just tell me who hired you," I say.

"You're one crazy fucker," he responds. "I'm a salesman."

"Not a very good one."

When I move closer he snarls. We're animals now. Somebody's going to get hurt. Somebody's going to get dominated. I fake a jab, he sidesteps and thrusts the fork like a tiny trident. I grab his wrist and he punches me square in the cheek. As I stumble backwards he pursues, trying to land his shoe on my thigh but coming up short. This has to happen fast. My fists become a flurry, a storm bombarding his face so he has to defend. His fork is useless as he covers his precious face, so I haul back to punch him in the balls.

He's too fast. Tongs sparkle in the snowy light filtering in through the window as they arc like a half-rainbow through space, seeking my eye. I'm about to get that scar I was dreaming about, and it wouldn't be so bad would it? But I might have to explain it on the way out, and that's not something I want. So I bail, wobble backward, and he lunges at me. He's got a bloody lip where one of my punches landed, and I have a feeble grasp on my balance. So I dodge to my left, trapping myself on his small bed. Fuck. I'm cornered! I grab the pillow as an anti-fork device. He laughs and stands guard with his hilarious little weapon. Best weapon in the room.

"You maniac," he says. "Now you're trapped. Is this how you get your kicks? Go on trains and beat up random people? Maybe that's what rich people do when they get bored at the top. Well you picked the wrong man this time."

There's no point wasting my breath by

talking to him now. I'll save that for later, after he submits. I crawl to the back of the single bunk and lift up the mattress. Push it forward between him and me. "Fuck off," he laughs, but then I rush him. Charging with the floppy mattress which is too big to outmanoeuvre.

"The fuck?" I hear him stumble as I shove the whole thing against the opposite wall. His feet stick out beneath the mattress and I stomp on his ankle, making him grunt. Next move? I grab those ankles and pull, making sure he falls horizontal beneath the mattress, which I jump on, to his dismay. Now, I can't beat him through the thick foam. So I stand up and jump on him with both feet, once, twice, and then he's scrambling to get out.

I have him. He's emerging frantically, like he was trapped inside a shell, face down. The fork is nowhere to be seen, and his face is all confusion as he tries to twist around and get free. I pin him down and Rusty moans like a sad trombone. His legs are still beneath the mattress, and now his upper body is beneath mine.

"I give up," he says, and I can feel his strong shoulders shrug beneath my right arm.

"Who hired you," I repeat. My satisfied voice is like a truck engine. "That's all I need to know. Then you won't need the beating I really want to give you."

His face is smushed on the carpet, one eye trying to look up at me. He has an awkward grin which is somewhat infuriating. "I'm a salesman," he says again, voice rising, momentarily frustrated at having to repeat himself. "My client is a company who salvages ship wrecks, and I'm looking for buyers."

He's lying and it pisses me off. He knows I'm in control. A couple slaps in the face turn his smirk into a snarl. I whisper in his ear, "Truth time, my newest friend. You invaded my life. I'm a forgiving man, when my plans are secure. But I've got a lot of cards in play, a lot of things in motion, and there is absolutely nothing I won't do to protect this project. Have you ever worked on something bigger than yourself? Have you ever conceived of an act that goes beyond merely making money? Boy, you're fucking with a force of nature."

He chuckles as much as his chest will allow with me on top of it. "No-one will fucking believe this," he says to himself. "Man, you got the wrong guy. I have no idea what you're-"

I cut him off with an elbow to the face. "Last chance," I tell him. "Then it's going to get ugly."

I realize my pulse is racing. The desire for violence and domination, to feel him suffer and submit, threatens to overwhelm any strategic thoughts. I've already given him more information than he's given me.

"It's a salvage company," he says again. "You already took the card."

Now I press my knee against his back, freeing my hands to throw off the mattress. I grab his balls and squeeze. He twists, tightens up. "I'll bust your goddamn testicle," I tell him, and find one, applying pressure.

"Fuck you," he whimpers, sounding defeated but refusing to give me the information I crave. Well I will take something else that I crave. The animal takes over. I take off my belt and tie his hands behind his back. I reach around, and undo his belt and pants button.

"What... what are you doing, man?"

I lay on top of him, and push myself against him so he knows the bounty that he is about to receive. Panicking, he scrambles to get up but I bash his face against the floor, and he slumps with a despairing moan. I pull down his pants, and then my own, and my weapon is ready for full domination. The animal is unleashed.

"I'll tell you anything man," he gasps, writhing uselessly.

But it's too late and I have no more words to say to him. My pulse blinds me, my victory overwhelms me, and I communicate everything to him in a physical way. A few thrusts and tears trickle down his face, but he never sobs. I can smell his sweat. I connect to an ancient thing. How many times has this happened? How many animals have mounted their prey? A few more thrusts, and he is pushing against me. Without words, without personality, after dignity is stripped away, he can find the place where he enjoys this. But the animal that has taken over cannot let him enjoy it too much. I push his face into the carpet and ride him harder, grabbing a handful of that perfect hair. My toes curl and I let out an animal roar for the few final thrusts, glorious supremacy expressed in the ultimate feeling of joy that a man can experience. I am a wolf as my spit flecks my beard.

My eyes are wide like a crazy person and I am panting as I stare down at the ruined thing beneath me. I am still inside him and I give one final wet push, but the joy is gone. No need to linger. I exit his body, and pull up my pants. We'll have to switch belts, since I'm not ready to untie him. He rolls over and trembles in a corner as I use my pillow to wipe the sweat off my face. Well, he won't give me any information now. In his desk I find his cell phone and a notepad. I check his text messages, but they have all been deleted. A suspicious act, indeed. So I check his contacts, glad to see that there are only a few, and I write down their names and numbers.

Ever the gentleman, I return the mattress to

its rightful place, and even fix the sheets. Then I sit and observe my defeated foe. "Why don't you call for help?" I ask him, already knowing the answer.

"What I'm selling isn't always legal," he hisses, still flustered, a piece of spittle falling onto his lip. The poor man is traumatized. Probably he was given a simple assignment, observe and report. He never expected this.

"I don't like being followed," I explain. "This incident is a warning. Do you understand?"

He laughs. "You have no idea how much I don't understand."

"Well now you can see that you've stepped into something bigger than yourself. Indeed, something bigger than myself and all my allies. Tell your boss to keep away from me. I promise it will get worse."

"You're fucking crazy."

"Indeed."

I quietly exit and head back to the restaurant car. I want rum so I order a double. Can I smoke a cigar? Of course not. We're inside a public space. Who is dominated now? Standing at the bar I observe the quiet crowd, allowing the animal to subside so I can be a man once more.

The train stops around dusk to pick up new passengers, and unload others. Among the waste it disposes is my defeated lover. I can see him out the window on the platform with his red jacket and sunglasses. His messy hair is not perfect anymore, but it is better than I left it. He came at me from the void, whole. I send him back crippled. He sees me from the corner of his eye and scowls as he limps away.

Back in my cabin, exhausted and ready for sleep, I admit to myself that I am ashamed. Not because I was too brutal to the man. Somebody is unfurling their tentacles into my business, and I will cut off those tentacles without hesitation. No, I am ashamed because I let my emotions control me. I aim to be a beast of a man, not a man-beast. This was a risky battle. If I were arrested, what would happen to the pieces of my grand puzzle? I am the coordinator, the one who strings the pieces together. I saw the whole plan in the stars, and only I connected the dots. I am collecting the pieces. I purchased the volcanic base, researched the best architects and engineers, hired the crack security team, and sought out all the necessary technology. This was years in the making, all under cover, the next logical step for the species and yet an untapped resource. I risked it all for the beat in my pulse. The sense of adventure. The joy of domination.

Then again, I needed to send a strong message. I needed to say, "Fuck off," to the underhanded weasels who are jealous of my greatness. And now I've done that. I wouldn't say that Rusty deserved to be fucked, but I would certainly say that he needed to be fucked. This is a high stakes game, and they will take me down if I show weakness or compassion. Strike me hard, friends! I'll butcher your families. It's necessary and right to unleash the beast. That's the path to victory.

So why do I still feel shame?

Because I am human.

I take the shame with my hard-earned victory, and I sleep.

Chapter 3

My only friends out here are the dead branches whipping past the windows, or the fields of snow. No. The truest friend is the rumble of this train which carries me north and west to my daughter, my home, and the living package that awaits me. So much to anticipate, but for now I am in the metal womb, not eager to be born but instead comfortable in my respite.

Finally, after I have slept and read and eaten my fill, I exit the womb at a remote train station beneath the imposing Rocky Mountains, where my rugged Jeep awaits in long-term parking. Of course I check the machine for any signs of tampering. I can't be too careful considering the numerous recent intrusions. Then I take hold of my own transportation at last and venture into the foothills on a lonely old road with scant trees. The pavement is faded, yellow lines barely visible. Hunters pass me on the way back from their trip. Were they successful? I cannot see into the covered back.

I leave the pavement and take a dirt road which leads into the evergreens. I can smell them even with the windows closed. The road is bumpy and I take it slow, watching for any obstruction. These dirt roads feel so temporary, with nature eager to fill them in with new growth. Coniferous needles crowd the way, reaching out to each other across the path like a family split apart by the oppressive regime of humankind. I drive between them in my miniature tank and they scrape at the hull as the Jeep bellows smoke for them to consume.

The next road takes me onto my private property. In the mountain far above I can barely see the glint of waterfall beside my house, which is built into the solid rock. The house is just below a small waterfall, but just above a much larger one. Also visible are sections of the zig zag trail these wheels must traverse to reach that lonely embedded abode. Zig zags are necessary as the hill is to steep to mount directly.

Finally I am home. I round that final corner where I can see the little valley, like God herself dug a chunk out of the mountain so I could build a house in the cozy corner. The mountain rises further and further in ascending peaks, the vibrant green eventually giving way to stark stone and white tips. But right here we have a small waterfall crashing down from above, pooling into a serene lake, before rushing again down to further layers of rapids and a much deeper waterfall below. My home is built into the cliff, just to the right of that smaller waterfall. The dark wood siding reflects off the unfrozen portions of the lake. A long deck runs in front of it, crawling along the rock and beneath the waterfall. Further on the deck leads to stairs which disappear down the hillside, where one might enjoy my network of trails. The windows of my house look down over the lake and the cliff beyond. I squint at the window to see if Stephanie is watching for me, but there is nobody. She must be studying. It's getting late, so I hope she's not still outside somewhere.

I park the Jeep and savour the crunch of my shoes on the gravel. Now I'm a man out of place, fine clothes in the cold wilderness. I'll have to change soon, and tomorrow go for a long refreshing hike. But tonight I will catch up with my daughter, and make sure her attitude hasn't spoiled in my absence.

I keep a small staff here and they will know that I've arrived. They're expecting me anyway, but they will have seen the images of the brown Jeep snapped by hidden cameras along the road, transmitted via underground wire to the small security station. The only thing that greets me is the roar of my waterfall, and the icy spires that hang from that ledge. My lake is ringed with a thin layer of ice, broken at each end where the water flows in and out. I breathe in my frosty air and behold the small valley. At lower altitudes winter brings decay, but only hearty evergreens grow up here. At higher altitudes only shrubs survive. Valhalla is halfway up a mountain.

The same paranoia that made me check my car for explosives inspires a vision of treachery invading the layers and tunnels of my mountain home. When I can't see the source of my aggressor, I can't accurately predict his manifestations. So I keep my eyes and ears open.

The front door is locked, so I punch in the security code and let myself in. My home is a vast cabin, even if it is built inside a cave. The floor and the walls are pine, and great bearskin rugs decorate the floor. My security man, Wallace Hooke, sits cross legged in my reading chair reading as if he were me. On the right wall the fireplace is a good distance from the large-screen television. Behind all this, a long wooden hand-crafted table separates the living room from the kitchen, where my lovely daughter is preparing a meal.

"Hi daddy," she says casually. "Welcome home."

"That smells damn good," I tell her truthfully. Whatever she's roasting, the juices are soaking my brain. "What is it?"

"Eagle."

I look at Wallace. "You let her hunt eagles again?"

Wallace puts a bookmark between the pages and rests the hardcover tome upon his knee. His eyes are as dark as his slick hair and as steady as his slight grin. He could almost be my son, and I almost think of him as such. "No. But she does it anyway."

"You want him to wrestle the bow from me, daddy?" She challenges me with her hazel eyes. She looks like her mother but she acts like me.

"Has she been studying at all?" I ask Wallace.

"Hardly," he tells me. "She's degenerating into a mountain-woman. She has her own smaller cabin built further up the mountain now, built with her own hands."

I nod. This is what I expected. But I have just arrived, and an argument about the girl's lifestyle would be ineffective from this platform. Instead, I remove my shoes and cross the room to kiss her cheek. She's wearing an apron and her light brown hair is pulled back in a ponytail. Then I head down the hall to change into something more comfortable. Jeans and a thick sweater, wool socks. When I return, dinner is ready at the table. Wallace sits with us, but the other security men are on duty. We'll save some for them. The meat must have been roasting for hours, it's so tender and juicy. My tongue studies the flavours, trying to discover what the mighty eagle feasted on before my progeny felled him. And in my heart I say a silent prayer, not to any vague deity but to the eagle himself, to accompany the transference of his nourishment into my veins and muscles.

"The spirit of the eagle fills our souls," Stephanie says, almost a prayer. I wonder if it is the job of a parent to clip his child's wings, or provide the wind beneath them. She cannot experience a rich life if she stays on a mountain.

"You have two degrees," I remind her. "But you live like a caveman."

"Cavemen didn't have composite bows, martial arts training, GPS, or billionaire globe-trotting fathers."

"What about your PhD? What about being involved in the technical details of world-scale projects? Does my daughter lack ambition?" I try to pin her down with me stone-heavy eyes, a gaze that breaks men, to show her the depth I've accumulated out in the world, a world that can be hers. But instead her own pin me to the wall like I'm a flimsy butterfly.

She presumptuously explains to me the psychology of high-level humans. "There's passion, and there's *a passion*. There's ambition, and there are specific goals. I have an infinite supply, daddy. I'm percolating. If you want me involved in business, you could involve me in yours. Some kids don't want the family business, but I do."

I shake my head. "I'm blinded by love. I can't effectively use you, because I can't fire you. I hire people because they prove themselves, not because they're my family. I provide you with resources and training, you provide your own path. Ideas come from out in the world, and character comes from hard work. This is your land, but remember that there's no path out here."

"Yes daddy," she says mockingly, and I pity whoever she marries, if she ever submits herself to the bonds of matrimony.

I turn my attention to business, and Wallace. "Has a package arrived for me?"

He nods. "It's waiting in the basement, along with some notes from Alex."

"Have the men bring it out to the ledge."

"What's in the package?" Stephanie asks. "I saw the helicopter, carrying a wooden box."

"A failed infiltration device."

And soon I go to meet this failure. My virus. I follow a short underground tunnel which takes me out to a natural ledge on the face of the deeper cliff below my home. When I stand on this ledge looking out, the waterfall crashes from above and to my left, spraying me slightly and creating an icy slick on the flat stone. From here we can watch the torrent of droplets tumble violently to the ice and rocks below before swishing on down the river in relative peace. There's no sign of my home from this vantage point, or any human habitation. Just the purity of nature spread out below me.

"What a view!" I declare to the package that awaits me. She is a woman, wearing slacks and a blue shirt. A brown sack covers her head so she can hear me, but she can't see me. Her white fingers clutch the arm of the wooden chair to which she is tied. The legs of the chair are so close to the icy edge that if she shuffles around she will fall to her death. I pull off the sack to behold her shivering face. She has frightened eyes and hearty cheeks, dark hair which doesn't quite reach her shoulders. First she takes a look at me, warm in my bearskin cloak and fur ushanka, plus my wonderful beard and seal-skin gloves. Then she sees the waterfall and looks over the edge, and makes a panicked sound in her throat before regaining her composure. That side of her is wet from the slight spray.

"Lucky you can't see behind you," I tell her. "And the hundreds of feet you could fall if you squirm too much on this icy rock!"

This makes her squirm, and I can hear the rickety wood of the old chair creaking even above the rush of waterfall noise. "Monsieur, je ne parle-"

"Cut the shit, Maude," I instruct her. Alex's info sheet identified her as Maude Benoit. "English. Don't fuck this up. I sent a message to your boss already when I caught someone following me, but I'm ready to send a stronger one. If you give me the information I need then I can trust you to bring information back to whoever hired you. First things first. What were you doing on my property?"

"Monsieur, I was just taking pictures, I promise you. Your guards, they catch me and take my camera. I could not share any information, I did not have time. Though I now see your face, I do not know your name. You have no fear from me!"

"It was a digital camera and you may have sent those pictures before you were caught," I speculate, though Alex's notes dictated that this is not true. "And my name is Julius Maxwell Cinnamon, so now you know. I sell cinnamon, real estate, and raw materials, and I have my fingers in many pies. I understand, you bear no ill will for me and my ventures. Am I right?"

She nods vigorously with wide eyes. Lips tremble with the cold. "Absolument monsieur! We can all get along."

"So, why were you inside my compound? Why were you taking pictures of the drilling site and the facility?"

"The location, it was delivered to me. They hired me to find info about the property. Just pictures, and they paid me good money."

"Who hired you?"

A stray spray of water splashes the French woman's face and she grits her teeth against the cold of it. "It is so cold, bring me inside please!"

I shake my head. "I need to find out who is following me and spying on me. You've seen the scope of my project, so you know that I'm a very serious man. Just tell me his name."

Now it is her turn to shake her head, this time in despair. "I do not know."

I kneel down to look up into her defeated face. I am looking for an excuse to let her live. "You don't know who he is, so how can I use you to send a message back to him?"

Now she gets excited, though she should know better. "An email address he gave me, to send the pictures! I can tell you, and you write it down."

I tap my head and say, "It's recorded all up here." I seem to mean my brain, but actually there is a recording device in my hat. I will study this conversation later, in case I miss something the first time. So she eagerly recites the email address, nice and clear.

"What else?" I can see her wrack her brain, searching for anything that might stave off her doom.

"The money!" she says. "They paid me half up front. I can give you-"

I'm grimacing as I stand up. "No thanks. What else?"

I grab the back of the chair, push to tilt her slightly backwards as she gasps. Then I twirl her around so only one chair-leg is resting on the stone. The rest of her hangs over the precipice. She wriggles in the ropes that bind her to the wooden chair, which groans under her weight. The fearful sound that escapes her throat could almost be mistaken for an orgasm.

"Think hard, *mon amis*," I suggest. "How did he contact you? What exactly did he want you to find out about me? A name, a country. Tell me what they said."

"My forum online," she says, panting now, staring morbidly down at her doom. "Clients contact me there, and it is anonymous. He asks me only for pictures, simple message, gives me GPS location, pays in bitcoin."

"If it's your forum it's not really anonymous, is it? You must have their meta data, their IP address, something."

"A password," she says suddenly. "I remember their password for the forum."

This bores me. The last thing in the world that I care about is a password for a forum. I sigh: "What is it?"

"Blackburn!"

My hand grips the chair, an automatic reaction. Why am I hearing this name again, so soon after Victor hurled it at me, when I haven't heard it uttered in years. I whip her around and stare into her face. The wind whips her hair as it blows my cloak. I stare into her frightened eyes, not knowing what to ask.

"Is it important?"

"Yes," I say with a smile. "So important. And very strange."

She smiles back, and a tear runs down her cheek. "But that is all I know monsieur."

"That's too bad," I tell her. She has failed to transform herself into an asset. I hook my foot beneath the rung of the chair and tilt her backwards. Her eyes and mouth pop open in a triangle of fear. Her hair blows across her face as she tips beyond the point of no return, gravity pulling her down off the perch.

I don't watch her fall. No need to see a pretty woman smashed on the rocks. I consider taking a picture though, and sending it to Victor. And I wonder about her last few moments as she tumbles through the air. Can she find peace in this short fall?

That's two enemies thwarted, and I have a clue. I want to confront Victor immediately, but I cannot do that without proof, or at least some evidence to link him to these infiltrations. And I have other tasks which require my attention. Almost on queue, my phone buzzes an announcement. A text message has arrived from Armand. My contact from The Technical University of Sunderwich has chosen a time to meet me for the sale. My nanobots are ready.

I head back inside for some rum, and to play Scrabble with my daughter.

Chapter 4

This morning my body aches for a workout. These trips always disrupt my routine, so I'll give a little extra today. I pump iron in my private gym, sweat gushing from my pores and Slayer blasting cosmic warfare thunder from massive speakers that are taller than me. Breakfast of leftover eagle and sweet potato. Stephanie is already gone into the woods, hunting or building or hiking, lord only knows.

From my safe I gather bundles of cash and

pack it neatly into a brown suitcase, padding the leftover space with a layer of foam. A text message informs me that my helicopter has arrived. I dress in checkered slacks, a white shirt and suspenders with a bow-tie, and a red velvet jacket. Knives and small pistols adorn my body. Spiral stairs lead me up to the helicopter pad where Wallace is waiting, helicopter-wind blowing his hair and the jacket of his suit. Wallace climbs into the front seat beside the pilot. I climb into the back with Paul, one of the biologists I've hired for the project.

Liftoff. Here we go. The mountain drops away below and my world becomes a snow-frosted sprawl of tree-infested landscape. Paul wears a plaid suit, which works well with his undercut fluff of curly brown hair and dark-rimmed glasses to create a truly modern nerd-classic ensemble. A large case rests by his feet, and it looks heavy. "Is that the microscope?" I ask him.

Paul nods. "I can't wait to get a look at that nanotech," he says with enthusiasm, eyebrows and hands everywhere. "I almost feel bad for taking it from them, after the university invested so much in its development. But if they're just planning to sell it in the corporate world anyway, then fuck em!"

"It's not in our hands yet," I remind him. I want him to stay calm and focused, but I have to admit that the excitement is getting to me too. If this technology does what it's supposed to it's the last piece of the puzzle we need to get Agartha running. And with the events of the past two days, I can't simply expect the trade to go smoothly.

We land to refuel and Paul has to use the bathroom. I run through the routine with Wallace while we stretch our legs, but it's still hours away. Then it's back up in the air and across the border. My pilot calls in our expensive clearance. Wallace calls a taxi before the chopper lets us off in a field outside Sunderwich, WA. We book a motel room, and then head out for a meal before the meeting.

It's snowing when we arrive at the zoo. They shut down at six and we arrive at seven, after dark. The imposing steel gate is unlocked, as promised, and we file through. We all get snow on our tuques from the big flakes that wander down in the occasional cones of lamp-light. The broad paved walkways are empty, as are the animal enclosures. There are no footprints in the fresh snow, and I can't see anybody wandering around or hiding in the trees or bushes. That's good. The aquarium is a round, domed building whose doors are also left unlocked for us. Once inside I lead the way down some stairs until we are in a long hallway with a cement wall on the left and a glass wall on the right. The glass wall holds back the enormous body of water, where I watch a school of glistening fish part for a squid whose waving tentacles propel him through the murky liquid. I think he's looking at me.

The more interesting specimens stand at the far end of the tunnel. Three men, as promised, to match my own. I can only see their silhouettes from here, a chubby guy flanked by two leaner men. They wait for us and I see that Blake Elliot, my contact, has a fluffy brown moustache and smooth skin on his round, pale face. Brown plaid sweater, red ski jacket, tan boots. His friends wear black ninja-gear with only their faces exposed. He's clearly happy to be here, smiling as he holds onto the canister full of bleeding edge microscopic machines, molecules engineered to transform substances in an act of futuristic alchemy. I give him my best hunters' glare, a warning not to fuck me on this deal, and his sparkling eyes show no fear. He's either smart and this act will be smooth, or he's belligerent and somebody will get hurt. In the tank beside us the squid lashes open its tentacles to envelope a little white and black fish, sucking the swimmer into its hidden maw. Something larger moves way back, deeper in the depths, but it's too dark to see.

No words are necessary. I unlock the suitcase and display the crisp stacks of American dollars. Then I snap it shut and set it on the ground in front of me as Blake hands the canister to Paul. Wallace regards everything with vigilant stoicism, aware of the hostility of the world and prepared for murder. My hands too are very close to my tools of death and dismemberment. A deep part of me is eager to use them, just waiting for an excuse.

Paul kneels down with the canister beside his microscope case. He opens the can and his mini lab and starts fiddling with instruments. Blake has taken the money and is now checking the stacks to ensure that they're the real deal. The money is real. I like clean deals and strong foundations.

"Paul?" I say, not looking at him, but peripherally I can see him peering through the microscope's eyepiece.

"It's good, boss," Paul confirms, and deftly begins packing it up.

Blake's continued smile makes me suspicious. He nods and speaks his only word during the meeting: "Pleasure." Now he's backing away with his friends, up the opposite stairs. Paul hands me the canister. It has a nylon strap which allows me to sling it over my shoulder.

We have to cross the aquarium again before we're in the stairs. Nobody speaks, but the excitement is palpable. "Slow down," I remind them. Really it's Paul I'm reminding. Wallace is a pro. "Nothing's cool till we're back in the helicopter."

Wallace leads us up the stairs and pushes the door open. The snow is still falling and no new footprints mar the pavement nearby. He takes a step outside, lamplight from above showing me the pale plane of his smooth jaw. Now we're all crossing the pavement faster than before, following our footprints back to the exit. Enemies could be hiding anywhere. Up in a tree, inside that garbage can, beneath that pile of leaves. The layer of snow helps to show that nobody's been moving around on the ground recently. I feel like I'm inside a snow globe.

A gust of wind whooshes cold air across my face, and something dark catches my eye. I twirl around to see a shadow swarm over Wallace. The flash of a blade, and his throat is already gushing blood into the snow. My pistol is in my hands and I fire shots, little intrusive explosions which break the precious silence, but they go wide as another set of hands drags me to the ground from behind. The last thing I see while I'm still vertical is Paul staring down at his chest, where a knife perforates his sweater, turning it red.

My own attackers pull me down. Instead of resisting I leap backwards to unbalance them and perform a backwards roll, pushing off with my hands to land in a crouch. Either my pistol will find targets, or I'll bolt for freedom. Neither of these dreams come true. The whip-crack of a wooden weapon explodes unto my wrists, which nearly go numb and I struggle to hold my grip. I try to run but somebody's boot connects with my cheek and hammers my head backward. I am reeling. Looking for my attackers, wonderful experts who remain unseen. I must at least give them a good fight!

Knives will be more useful here than this foolish gun. With one gesture I return it to its holster and draw out two graphite blades. But somebody has found my feet and they pull them out from beneath me. All my weight topples forward and I'm face-down in the snow. My arms are pulled up behind me, twisted hard by someone of equal strength. I am defeated. The end will be soon. I wait for the knife that will sink into my heart or throat.

Instead I see boots. They are Blake's tan boots, and I look up into the face of the double-crossing scoundrel who murdered my men. He is, of course, grinning down at me. Somebody hands him the canister. My precious nanobots, denied me! Unless...

"Treacherous faggot," I snarl.

He puts his boot on my face and wipes the dirt off on my beard. It stinks like shit. He has stepped in shit and smeared it on his defeated enemy. Now he crouches over me, dangling a piece of paper. "There's one way you can survive this," he tells me. "Your property in Africa. Sign it over right now, and we'll let you walk away."

"How do you know about that?"

"Does it matter? Somebody is very interested in that piece of land, and I agreed to help them get it from you. It would be a shame to make an orphan of your beautiful daughter. Just sign the property over to my new friend, and you can go back to Canada where you belong."

"Well I can't sign anything with my hands pinned behind my back."

"My men will let you up, but if you try anything I'll fill your guts with bullets. Understand, shit-face?"

I laugh at his cleverness. "I think I got it."

They pull me up onto my knees. I'm surrounded by ninjas. Four in total, unless others are hidden elsewhere. With one hand Blake extends to me the contract he believes will earn him Agartha, on a clipboard with a pen clamped to the top. His other hand aims his pistol at me. His smug face is so sure that he's bested me. So proud, having made a deal, he thinks he's a criminal. I could grab this clipboard and shove the pen in his eye before he had a chance to fire his weapon, but I've already wrestled with his crew and I have no doubt they would take me down. So I calmly accept the clipboard, to buy time, and resist the urge to look up into the trees. They should have killed me when they had the element of surprise.

I pretend to read the contract and Blake says, "No need to read the fine print! You're signing under duress anyway. We're not drawing a second draft!"

I sign my name at the bottom. And to my right, a ninja's head ejects a spray of blood as he collapses forward. A similar fate befalls the man behind me. I've been hoping for this, but my captors are caught off guard. I jab the pen into Blake's wrist, ragged wound, and he drops the gun as I lunge after the third ninja. We spar, with me on the offensive. He blocks everything I throw at him, but then we're locked in an embrace, and I overpower him. Take him to the snow to test our ground game. My well-trained opponent is wriggly and flexible, but I am just as skilled and steady as a rock. I manipulate his body, get him in an arm guard, and snap the bone at the elbow as he shrieks. Moments later I mount him from behind and twist his neck until it snaps.

Only now can I take a good look around to see that the fourth ninja has fled, and so has Blake with my nanobots. I look for footprints in the snow. The fourth ninja seems to have gone over the fence, and if he's smart he'll stay gone. Blake, not athletic enough for such a feat, has fled across the zoo. I need only to follow those footprints, and the splatters of blood from his wounded wrist.

I keep my eyes open and a weapon in each hand. There could be others ready to take me down. Blake's trail leads around the aquarium, a clear trail in the growing layer of fluffy white. As I reach the opposite side, where the pavement leads to the opposite gate, I see two figures. Armand stands over Blake, who shivers and sobs on all fours. Blood pours from his nose and his face is badly battered. Armand has the nanobots in one hand, and a rifle in the other. When he sees me he raises the canister in salute. I wave back.

"I could not save the others," Armand explains. "The ninjas. They move too fast."

I nod. "I know. That was some good shooting. You never saw them come in?"

"I hide in the trees all day, my friend. I was a poacher and a child soldier, and nothing escapes my eye. But these ninjas, I did not see until it was too late."

I accept the canister of nanotech and clap my man on the shoulder. "Thank you, Armand."

"You want me to kill this rat?" He asks, kicking Blake hard in the ribs with an audible whump, making the man crumple up and groan on the ground like a slug.

I shake my head and walk around the wounded animal. "No. But there are two things I want from him. Blake, sit up."

He gets up on his knees and I say, "Give me that jacket."

He removes the jacket and offers it to me. I take it and throw it behind me. "Now give me your sweater."

He hesitates, giving me a funny look. I say, "I'll rip your lips off, fatso. Take off the goddamn sweater."

He pulls the garment over his head and hands it to me with trembling hands. I use the thick wool to wipe the shit from my beard. I get the bulk of it out, but the rest is now embedded even deeper. Drop the sweater on the ground. I recall my recent acts of brutality. I should have saved it all for this guy. Murderer and shit-smear, double crosser. I grin at him. "Tell me everything," I command. "How did you know about my African property, and who paid you to double cross me?"

After some stammering he blubbers out the truth. "A-after you guys m-made your offer, to buy the na-na-nanobots from my lab... a man came to my house. He offered me m-m-money and m-m-men. Black hair. Maybe th-thirty years old?"

"Does he have a name?"

Blake shakes his head. "He wouldn't tell me. But the c-company... it's on the c-contract."

I look at the signed paper, which I'd stuck in my pocket. I appear to have signed the property over to Jasserty Holdings Inc. "Good thing nobody will ever see this contract," I said, stuffing it back in my pocket. Then I look at Armand. "Somebody must have been following you already when you went to meet him."

Armand inclines his head, a half nod which shows me his shame at being so easily tailed. "Let me kill this man," Armand says. "He has infiltrated our business, when we were so good and trusting to him."

I shake my head again. "He's going to clean up this mess, with all the bodies. Maybe his good friend Sam will kill him for us. Where's the suitcase with the money?"

Blake nods toward the gate, where the case accumulates a pretty layer of snowflakes. I walk over and pick it up. Armand says, "What next, boss?"

"We get the microscope and we get the fuck out of here. Blake, if this comes back to me you have no concept of how bad I'll fuck you up. The only reason I'm leaving you alive is to clean up this mess. You had plans for my friends' corpses after you killed them. Now you've just got a couple extra corpses to deal with."

Later on Armand and me climb into the helicopter, and it's almost midnight. The pilot says, "The others?"

I shake my head, cradling the hard-earned nanotech in my arms. Despite my deep-rooted trust and my love for the man, I wonder if Armand Urbain is involved in these plots. But no, he tipped me off to Rusty when the blonde man followed me to the train. And he shot dead those ninjas, rescuing me from losing the canister. His loyalty is secure. Still, redundancy has saved me more than once. So I take out the tracking device from my lapel and place it inside the cap of the canister while Armand is not looking.

As the helicopter lifts off, the pilot says, "You smell like shit, boss."

Chapter 5

We approach Agartha.

I admit she is a humble volcano, neither huge nor active. The jungle rises halfway up the lone earthy breast, the wide brown tip open for penetration by helicopter. She is surrounded by the endlessly lush African wilderness. There are no villages in sight from this vantage point, and only one lonely road cutting through the trees and disappearing into the green hills and mountains beyond. The only human activity is the farm at the base of the volcano, worked by my employees. The farm feeds the small, hidden Negro army that surrounds and protects the dormant volcano and its inhabitants. This is a remote location. I feel as if God preserved this spot to be the womb for mankind's next incarnation. From above one would never guess what lays hidden below. Any buildings built on the volcano's surface are embedded into the slope of the small, conical mountain, and hidden beneath a canopy of dirt and junglebrush. These also serve as entryways into the interior complex of my underground retreat.

Armand is no longer with me. He went to collect the last batch of engineers, and should be bringing them here to meet me soon. An airplane brought me to Africa, after a shower and change of clothes, and a helicopter is now delivering me to the Congo.

I love to see all the things that can grow from the dirt. Volcanoes expel nutrients which by various molecular processes are transformed into grass, trees, worms, and men. We are trapped in an intricate molecular tapestry, the food chain. I hold tight to my canister of nanobots, not really bots at all but molecules specially engineered to harness and aggressively streamline those processes which collect and separate the ingredients for life from rocks and dirt.

Into the hole we go, a vertical descent into the womb of Agartha. My womb. The Earth's womb, via helicopter bearing the seed of me and my nanobots. Once inside there is no mistaking the advanced nature of this project. Where the volcanic orifice was once a shallow, ragged-edged bowl, I had it dug more than 200 meters deep in a neat cylinder. A spiral walkway is threaded down the cylinder's walls like the hole for a bolt. The walkway protrudes from the wall, as wide as a road, offering access to the many doors into the compound's interior. These doors in the curved rock wall lead to laboratories, greenhouses, living quarters, production facilities, and everything else a scientific community needs to exist independently. A network of tunnels connects everything in an unseen matrix within the rock which extends outward to the volcano's external slope.

My pilot lands deftly on a helipad, one of several which extend from the spiralling road at staggered intervals down the hole. I jump out the door, wearing a black turtleneck and charcoal grey slacks. The nanobot canister is slung over my shoulder. Like an awestruck child I must always run to the edge and peer down to the bottom when I arrive, to take a look at the vast tubes and metal buildings which comprise the geothermal energy processing plant. Of course only a portion of it is visible, with the injection wells coming in at an angle from the outside, and the generator and experimental batteries hidden from view in a nearby tunnel. Plus the primal energy of the molten earth deep below which powers the turbines, which we capture in our batteries.

Alex and Yrja await with a buggy and driver. Alex White is my security man inside the complex, with his mercenary guards and military experience at my disposal. They are separate from the native army that stands guard outside. His mangy red hair wraps all around his face, scraggly beard to wavy locks. He is wiry and pale, his eyes fierce. Yrja Ek is my Chief Science Officer and she runs the place in my absence. She looks more like an Aryan athlete than a scientist. Her blonde hair is tied back and she wears blue knee-shorts and knee-high socks above her black sneakers. Her sleeveless white shirt displays the tattoo covering her left arm. It is a great eye inside a pentagram, with other occult symbols branching out in a mandala that covers her whole upper arm. Utterly gorgeous, it's a shame her engineer-husband Bjorn works here too. Alex smokes a cigarette while Yrja holds a clipboard. They both greet me with a smile when I approach.

"Any more problems with intruders?" I ask Alex.

"Nah," the Scotsman rasps. "And these boring nerds are all mild as fuck. Did you learn anything from the girl I sent you? The photographer who snuck onto the mountain?"

I shake my head. "Not much." I don't want to share the name Blackburn with him, at least not yet, until I get more information myself. Alex handles interior security, not spying and external detective work. "But I've had other incidents. A man followed me on the train, who I utterly humiliated and sent running. And, much worse, somebody got to the man who sold me these nanobots. He murdered Paul and Wallace, and I had to let him live so he could clean up the mess. Somebody's got their teeth into us. I've fought off every attack so far, but I bet they're not finished."

"Argh," Alex spits on the floor, a distasteful act to express his disgust at our meddling opponent. When I give him a hard look he grumbles again and scrapes the spit around with his boot, as if that cleans it up.

"We needed Paul," Yrja says. "Now his blood is on my hands." She had personally recruited him from one of her previous projects. Her sharp features, her lips and jaw, arms and eyebrows, are all animated sharply when she speaks, like she's convulsing in concise little spasms.

"We wanted Paul, and we mourn his loss," I say, thinking more of Wallace, my personal guard and family friend. "We can reproduce these nanobots and get production started without him, but I promise to crush the fuckers who brought this on our heads."

Her sharp nod and piercing blue eyes tell me that she'll hold me to that promise.

The buggy carries us down the spiral road, past all the rooms dug into the wall. In a classroom dozens of young Congolese study, as part of a promise I made to the locals. I peer into a large laboratory where a lone scientist leans over his microscope. But most of the rooms are empty and dark, since full power is not ready to go online yet. But soon.

"How long until the first battery is full?" I ask Yrja. The generator's deep hum grows louder as the whining buggy takes us deeper.

"It is full," she says. I've relinquished the nanobots to her and the canister is slung over her shoulder. "We just need to detach it and roll it out. We decided to wait for you."

I'm glad she waited. "This is a grim day, since we lost allies and friends. But it's also a great day. I would say the official opening of this experiment. When the power goes online and the last of our most important scientists arrive, we can finally sink our teeth into the work which will occupy us for years, or the rest of our lives."

We pass the gym, where several people are running on treadmills or lifting weights, and my muscles ache for a workout.

The slope ends and the driver parks. Just as I had looked down from the top, now I must gaze up at the sky from the floor. A small and distant blue coin. I am deep inside the Earth, inside a special and secret place. There is a framework of pride in my perspective as I gaze at this thing I've created, but that framework is built on a mystical foundation of appreciation for my species and the very physical structure of the planet. Deep inside is where we all are, and I long for this claustrophobic cocoon. The things we will develop here, free from interference or dependence on the economic system, free from government regulation, will finally set free the individual and the species. Post-scarcity and trans-humanism are the destiny of the human race, but neither corporations nor governments are able to grasp it. The glorious responsibility falls on me.

Alex spits again and then rubs it out with his foot. I let it slide, but I will speak to him later about setting a good example. One of his guards stands outside the door to the domed generator room, as large as a house. I recognize the guard as Alex's younger brother Gavin, whose hair is somehow even more red than Alex's. He is clean-shaven, skin smooth as a baby's pussy, and that red hair is perfectly parted and trimmed which seems somehow absurd. How can you tame fire? They share a nod, and I'm glad to see the camaraderie. I wonder if I wish that I too had a brother. The hum of the generator is oppressively loud down here, and we all put in some earplugs.

Great tubes lead into a tunnel, wide as a hangar, dug into the wall. It is dimly lit by small overhead lights. Yrja leads us through the tunnel where my four experimental Ultimate Batteries await. They are cubes of black metal, as large as sheds, and they rest in a row on a train track which leads deeper into the tunnel's darkness. These imposing monstrosities are essential for Agartha's long-term functioning. They tower above me like religious icons, like Mecca or the Monolith, silent but full of energy. Well, one of them is full of energy.

"A whole year," I say with awe, shaking my head as I behold the cube on the far right, furthest from the entrance. Tubes likes tentacles reach out from the generator, pass over the three other batteries, and are plugged into the top surface of the fourth one. We're charging one at a time, starting on the right.

"A year to charge," Yrja repeats, "for ten years of power!"

Then she mutters something in Swedish into her phone, and soon men appear with ladders. They are climbing over my ultimate battery and detaching the tubes. They use remote controls to roll the batteries over to the right on the tracks, so they can begin charging the next one. The charged unit continues rolling down the track, where it will be plugged into Agartha's power grid elsewhere, at the end of the track, outside of the tunnels. The material is volatile, and while it is highly unlikely, such an explosion here at the base beneath the city could destabilize the whole structure. So it will be plugged in outside on the surface, where it can do less damage. I believe in redundancy.

I want to go and see it get plugged in. I want to personally flip the switch, but as we follow its trip down the track I get a text message from Armand. He has arrived with the scientists and I decide I'd like to inaugurate their arrival with a tour which will end with the battery, and my personal summoning of the god of electricity.

"Let's go meet our new colleagues," I tell Yrja and Alex. "Tell your men not to turn on the battery yet. I want the new scientists to be there when I do it." It will feel symbolic, that their first day here is the first day of a fully-powered Agartha.

Back in the buggy and back up the spiral roadway, I see helicopters fly away up out of the hole. These are the choppers that have delivered the crucial payload of my highly-skilled personnel. Armand will have gathered them all together on one helipad to meet their master. Twenty-five new men and women, if they all honoured their agreements. And here they are, my new colleagues, clustered around and talking all over the helipad. I tell the buggy driver to drive into their midst and they part like I am Moses. We park at the rail. Alex and Yrja climb out and face the crowd, but I climb up on the seat to get a good look at them all. Some of Alex's security men are here, too, and Armand, lanky and leaning on the rail, chatting up a dark-skinned *femme scientifique* with a great afro. There are more than twenty-five here. I recognize many faces and acknowledge happily that many of my existing team have come to greet the fresh minds. They range in age from early twenties to septuagenarian and I hold my hands out in a gesture of embrace for all the generations and ethnicities of scientist and engineer who have a grander vision than mere profit and prestige.

"Welcome!" I boom. "I haven't met you all, but I respect you all for taking on this bold and dangerous experiment. It will be a new way of life for all of us. Deep inside this African volcano, I must either appear to be a pretentious entrepreneur or a Bond villain. Soon you'll see that I'm neither, just a conduit for the vision that has brought you all here. You've left your existing work in Europe, Antarctica, America, Asia, all across the world to embark on this scientific adventure. From my own hard-earned fortune I've built facilities away from prying eyes and the capitalist system of funding and financial reward.

If we're self-sufficient we don't need to earn mere profits in somebody else's number-game. We will be free to pursue science for the sake of science, and science for the sake of the human race, but never for mere profit. Our species is running a race between post-scarcity and self-annihilation. It is the mandate of Agartha to encourage the former."

Alex spits, and scrapes it away with his boot.

I continue. "The economic system which has treated me so well is no longer a boon for the human race. While hippies whine about transforming the world's institutions, I seek to escape the Fermi Paradox and take you all with me! We begin with a single community based on science, art, and freedom through discipline. Our ultimate aim is to build a tool-set that humans can use to thrive in any environment. With that specific goal we can escape the multiform oppression of base economics, crude biology, and fickle nature."

Somebody calls out a question. "What kinds of technologies will be in the tool-set?"

I hold up my hand and count off items on my fingers. "Renewable energy, human cloning and genetic enhancements, revolutions in food production including the alchemy of nanotechnology, anti-gravity and space-flight, artificial intelligence, all this and more. We will live and breathe research and development. What you see here on the surface is the mere top-layer of my compound, our new home, where the laboratories and living spaces are dug deep into the very crust of the Earth. We are totally independent, producing our own food and electricity through various means, and we will develop more. You'll advance your learning in our classrooms, and you'll learn Martial Arts and survival skills, as our current inhabitants are already doing. We have the blessing of the Congolese people, who we are training as scientists and who protect us from invaders. We also mine precious metals, to use ourselves or to trade for outside goods and services."

Alex spits again, and I want to rip his jaw off, but I won't interrupt my speech. The beards, the smiles, the radiant faces of the interested crowd deserve my full attention at this moment. I can see all the pride of humanity, the ambition that only exists before economic factors reduce a man down to a slave, reflected in their faces. They are eager for my vision. I can give them the glory that lured them into the sciences in the first place.

"We have unique technologies on-site, and I'm counting on you to develop more. Some include the Rock Eaters, nanobots we can use to produce food from stone, which I have shamelessly stolen from a corrupt laboratory. Like Robin Hood,

I intend to develop this into a technology we can mass-produce and share with the poorest communities. I'll bring you on a tour which will end with my Ultimate Battery. This sweet battery is a special alloy, a giant cube of metal interlaced with a neural network of biological material which holds an enormous amount of energy, is programmable, and quite possibly sentient. It can absorb various kinds of energy, and deliver it as crisp electricity."

More buggies are arriving to turn this crowd into a caravan, so we can spiral down together and get a good look at the major parts of this vertical science-city.

I gesture at the blond Swede and tell the crowd, "This is Yrja Ek, our Chief Science Officer. I trust her with running this show, so you can trust her too. Her mind is sharp and her passion runs deep."

She waves to them, and I move on to Alex. "This is my security man, Alex White. His men will arrest you if you get into fights, but they'll also protect you from any evil-minded intruders that make it past our men on the outside."

Alex waves humbly at the gathered folks. He looks up at me as I smile down at him, and he spits in my face. The momentary surprise of his disgusting insult is just enough time for a knife to appear in his hand, which he slices through the air and jams deep into Yrja's belly. As I wipe the spit from my eye I realize that the buggies which arrived are not empty. They carry Alex's security men, and they block the exit from the helipad, carrying their semi-automatic weapons.

I was embarrassingly slow on the draw, but Yrja has caught Alex's hand before it can get all the way in. Blood already swells around the white fabric, but she screams in his face and head-butts him brutally three times in the nose which gushes red liquid. He stumbles backwards, releasing the knife, and she stalks after him with the weapon protruding like morbid jewelry from her lean belly. Before she can grab him, his men grab her and pull her back, taking the canister of nanobots first and handing it off. The crowd clusters together, shouting their surprise.

My moment of unforgivable confusion is over, and my primary concern is Yrja's safety. Two traitorous grey-clad guards hold her back while a third grabs the knife, and pushes it deeper into her organs. I fall on him with tremendous rage. I grab his throat to lift him up. Like a shot-putter I hurl the thin man through the air, and over the edge of the railing where he chokes from his injured throat, wailing hoarsely as he falls to his death. The two men who hold the struggling, bleeding scientist, now drag her to the edge, where they intend to toss her down to her own doom. I move to protect her, but rough hands pull me back. It is Alex and more of his guards, and they are too many and too strong. I look around for Armand but he is nowhere to be seen. Also missing is the tall lady he was chatting with. Has he abandoned me? Is he a traitor too?

With all my might I struggle to be free, roaring like a bear. Alex stands before me, grinning like a red-haired weasel and holding another goddamned piece of paper, and I know what he wants. "Sign it over," he instructs me. "I'll kill these nerds until you make me rich, I swear to fuck, you pretentious old billionaire."

I laugh at the petty injustice of small minds, staring up at the circle of sky. The sun is high noon, burning its radiation down like a hateful life-giving all-seeing eye. "Behold all that I've built and all that I've dreamed!" I scream at the heartless god who lays inside all things, exploding from the distant star. "Fucked by the petty minds of the worthless drooling faggots whose-"

A fist smashes my mouth to silence and I laugh. "Bottom-feeding trash," I snarl and glare at my enemy.

"Fine words," Alex says, and spits on the floor. "But my men have guns, and we like to get paid!"

"You're paid well," I remind him.

"Could always be better! My men are everywhere. You lost before you even started. I control the facility, and the nerds will do what I tell them if they want to live. Your nanobots will go back to their rightful owner, who has paid me better than you! You've got a big pie and there's a few folks who want a piece. I'm just the man to portion it out! You just need to sign the land over to my new boss, so the paperwork will check out if the government asks questions."

I laugh again. He understands so little. This place won't function under those conditions. He'll rip my dream apart for the small cash-grab and his new boss, whoever that is, will liquidate my assets and probably butcher all these scientists. This place is worth more than the sum of its parts. My mind searches for an escape route, but it seems that all is lost. I've foolishly trusted mercenaries with the protection of my beautiful project, and they've taken it from me by force. If only I could get a message outside, to the dark-skinned army who aren't under Alex's greedy command.

Somehow they haven't yet managed to finish murdering Yrja. As the two men struggle to throw her over the edge, she frees one arm and scratches out both the eyes of the soldier who holds the other. He drops to his knees and covers his bleeding face with both hands. Some of her hair has come loose, hanging in strands over her face. Enraged animal, she pulls free the knife in her gut, and the wound ejaculates blood. She wheels around, armed now, and proceeds to slash and stab at her other oppressor. When he falls, crying for forgiveness, she kneels over him and stabs his face, throat, and torso. Her screams are a nightmare, and tears of pride run down my face.

I see the pack of scientists and I wonder if they too may be a battery full of stored energy and potential. "Scientists!" I scream. "*KILL THEM ALL!*"

The dam bursts. Yelling nerds swarm the security men, who only hesitate for a frozen moment before opening fire. Scientists collapse, dying or clutching their wounds, but then guards are disarmed, and thrown over the railing. It's a noisy bloodbath as they wrestle and fight, although the newcomers are less eager than the few who have already made this place their home. I'm glad I introduced hand-to-hand combat into the fitness regimen. Every human should know how to use their body!

Fuelled by anger and surprise, Alex swoops in on me. "Look, I've got more men. You can't win this. Call them off or they'll all fuckin' die!"

But I just cheerfully hold his gaze as his men keep me subdued. Now the scientists have guns, and they're coming for Alex. More of the security guards arrive in buggies, and the scientists take bad shots, mostly missing. Bodies lay everywhere. I hear the flud flud noise of helicopters coming down from above. I hope they are somehow here to help me, but I know that they're not. Indeed, more of Alex's men dangle from ropes, hanging down and firing into the wailing crowd. But the crowd fires back, mostly missing but occasionally hitting their targets. Men fall to the helipad and break their legs. Others fall beyond, screaming to their violent deaths. Bullets hit the propellers and the machine wobbles.

Alex has frantic eyes which cast around in the chaos seeking answers. I tell him, "This is not how you planned it."

"Not how you planned it either," he retorts. Now he brandishes the contract again and I see that same name, Jasserty Holdings. I wonder if I will live long enough to find out who has done this to me.

Now the crowd is upon us, dwindled in numbers but not in motivation. The helicopter above is smoking from the bullets of my brave nerds. Unable to gain height, it spins out of control and crashes into the opposite walkway, propellers snapping to pieces against the cement which crumbles. Then it's tumbling down. I hope it doesn't destroy the generator at the bottom.

The second helicopter has followed bravely, but they're smart enough not to engage in a firefight. This black machine hovers just beyond the helipad and a man in a suit hangs out and screams, "The nanobots! Throw us the nanobots!"

One of the men who has been holding my arm has to use one hand to draw his pistol, firing into the crowd. I see an old man die as he tries to free me, but his death is not in vain. The soldier is distracted so I use all my weight to push and pull, bringing him off-balance until a fat man and a fat woman get a grip of the guard and begin to beat him. With one arm free I can fight the other man, but he lets go and runs. Good enough for me. Now I can murder Alex. But I see he's got the canister and he's running for the helicopter.

I pound the pavement to reach him first. A dive and a tackle brings him down like a football player clutching the pigskin. The man in the helicopter shouts again, "Throw the canister!"

"Help me!" Alex wails, unwilling to sacrifice himself for any other cause. I proceed to break his arm and smash his face on the pavement. I rip a chunk of his hair out of his head. I am a fucking monster and I will rip the traitor to pieces.

Yrja is stalking around with two bloody knives in her hands, slouching and bleeding from multiple stab wounds. My mob is dispersed, hiding behind buggies and trading fire with the enemy. Somebody is shooting at the helicopter. I realize I should be killing Alex, not just beating him, so I put my thumbs on his eyes and begin to push them into his skull.

A flash of light. Somebody has kicked me in the face. I reel and manage to grab their leg. They struggle to be free but I've got it tight, standing up, rushing her. She's a muscular woman, wearing the uniform of Alex's Traitors. With one arm I hold her boot and push backwards. My other fist slams down on her knee until it breaks backwards, and I throw her over the rail, and I am glad that she will die. But her plan has worked, she has freed Alex, and I see him climb into the helicopter which is lifting off even as more bullets pock the hull with a tinny rat-tat-tat noise.

I have no choice. I make a running leap, flinging myself like a squirrel from a branch and grab the landing skid among the rain of bullets as the chopper makes its wobbly ascent. I take one last look below and yell out to the scientists, "Hide! Make them draw out their mutiny! It's a civil war!" I can already see somebody helping Yrja get to safety, and a line of people are scurrying through the doorway to a darkened laboratory. One man stands firing ineffectual shots at me with his pistol. It is Alex's younger brother Gavin, and when he sees that I see him he points one ominous finger, marking me.

Harsh smoke fills my lungs and burns my eyes, causing a coughing fit that almost makes me lose my grip. Now we're high above and I can't let go, but the helicopter is tilting and wounded, smoking dangerously. The angle changes and I can breathe fresh air again. I gulp a big lungful, and pull myself up into the vehicle's open door. My torso is instantly shocked with bullets from a pistol, one, two, three into my chest, shoulder, and belly. But I am relentless and have no other course but to move forward, bleeding, to grab Alex as his wavering hand tries to shoot me again. He's in no condition for a fight, with the beating I gave him on the helipad. But I'm only just beginning to bleed. I have time to grab his gun, push it into his gut, and fire enough shots to open a big ragged hole. My hand goes into that hole and grabs a chunk of intestines. I pull it out as he wails like a bleeding baby, whining bitch, he sees his own guts and he knows the horrible consequences of his actions.

But I don't see the canister, and I don't see the man in the suit who was shouting at Alex previously. He must be the man who is now seated beside the pilot. I aim to climb up front, bloody hands and bleeding chest, and I see the man in the suit with a helmet on, so I can't see his face. The canister sits in his lap, and I aim the gun at his head.

Too late. The helicopter tips and I stumble

toward the exit. We're just rising out of the mouth of the volcano, skimming over the dry land at the very lip. An idea comes into my head, and I make a quick decision, a hard gamble. I could jump out now and survive. So I shoot past the pilot at the easier target: The control board. Empty the pistol, and leap out the door. Of course the drop is further than it looked. The pain is excruciating, the shock jarring, and I think I've broken some ribs. The helicopter may be in worse shape than me, though. I manage to lift myself up enough to see the machine spiralling out of control, still puffing smoke. My hope is that it will crash hard enough to kill the inhabitants, but not hard enough to destroy the canister and its precious contents.

But what is this? A third chopper, painted red and much heavier than the others, has escaped my notice until now. It has stolen equally precious cargo. Hanging by cables is my Ultimate Battery, freshly charged and freshly poached. This was a bold operation indeed, and thorough. The wounded helicopter finally crashes in a puff of smoke, raking the vegetation with is blades as it tumbles over and over in the rolling jungle beyond the mountain's base. The other chopper changes direction, heading to the crash site. I see it descend so the battery rests on the ground, and a rope tumbles from the open door. The man in the suit, canister lashed over his shoulder, climbs the rope, and the machine flies away.

My tired consciousness attempts to calculate the scarce information at-hand. They came to steal my nanobots, the Ultimate Battery, and my signature for the whole property. This makes me wonder if there must be two different parties involved, since there would be no point in stealing the battery and bots today if they thought I would sign over the whole thing anyway. I have clearly lost the nanobots and the charged battery, but I see dark-skinned men in green uniforms running up the hill toward where I lay, and I know that we can take back the volcano which Alex's men have stolen. The African soldiers kneel around me and speak worriedly in French.

"Monsieur Cinnamon! Vous êtes blessé!"

"Il est une mutinerie," I explain. "Les soldats de Alex sont assiégeaient les scientifiques à l'intérieur. Vous devez les aider! Trouvez Armand!"

One man speaks forcefully into a walkie talkie while the others insist on looking at my wounds. "Nous devons vous apporter chez le médecin," I am told. I nod my head in agreement. They help me stand, and now I can feel how much blood I have lost. The helicopter is receding in the distance. I lament that I am too weak to chase it.

I hear the sound of my cell phone in my pocket. Somebody has sent me a text message, but

I can't let go of my protectors without collapsing. "Mon téléphone dans ma poche," I utter. "Lire le message pour moi, s'il vous plaît."

They read to me some welcome good news. It is Armand, and he says he had taken a lady to a secret place to make love, when the mutiny went down. This is a suspicious coincidence, but I have no choice but to trust him. He says he has connected with his men on the outside, and now they will proceed to take back the compound from Alex's headless army.

Now they have Armand on the walkie talkie and I tell him what has been stolen.

"We will take back Agartha," Armand's voice declares through the earpiece. "You hunt down the men who did this, take back what they have stolen, and return to us!"

I promise that I will. And my soldiers lead me to their village, where their doctor will tend my wounds.

Chapter 6

The rich red road leads me away from my beloved Agartha and towards the unknown. I am wounded but healing, bandaged and travelling in the company of a fine troupe of five African soldiers. Our Jeep makes easy work of this level terrain and I relax in the open rear, looking back on the road behind us. My volcano has already disappeared in the distance. Not dressed so elegantly now, I wear the same loose green military-style uniform as my men, and carry the same AK-47. I try to peer into the jungle, the endless layers of leaves and grass, but it is impenetrable and I wonder how humans ever survived before we mass-produced machines. Yet I know that the jungle-beast still lives in my heart, the ferocious animal, himself hidden behind the leafy-layers of language and ideas which compose my modern manliness. Is the beast truly hiding? Or is he pulling the strings?

The beacon is still hidden in my nanobot-canister and I can track its location on my phone. To my delight, it has not left Africa. In fact it is still in the Congo, and nearby. Probably they are storing it temporarily at some secret location as they prepare another means of transportation. The helicopter alone cannot carry the massive cube of energy out of Africa. I may try to steal back the nanobots, if it seems feasible. But I mostly want to learn who is behind this usurpation and where they are going so I can plan a more organized assault, reclaim what is mine, and drain the life from my antagonist.

We have company. It is an armoured off-road vehicle, more sturdy than my own and driven by a man with perfectly parted red hair. Somehow some of Alex's men have made it out of Agartha and have come to revenge themselves upon me. "So be it," I say, and aim my machine gun at the wheels of the approaching Jeep. I spray bullets at the rolling rubber but my shot is untrue as my wounded shoulder is in a worse state than I thought. I can handle the pain that penetrates my flesh, but I am dismayed by the patter of wasted bullets which bounce off the vehicle's fender and fortified windshield. I cannot aim for shit with these wounds. There is steady hate in Gavin's eyes, and he pushes the truck even faster. I see other men in the truck with him.

In Gavin's eyes I can see my mistake. My colleagues at Agartha joined me out of passion. They took part in my vision regardless of money or prestige. They all wanted a better future for themselves and the species, and so they were loyal to my cause. Alex and his men worked only for money, mercenaries from a different world. I should never have employed anybody on those terms. Gavin's love for his gutted brother is more pure. He surely wants to kill me now, or at least finish the job of taking Agartha for his family. They have their loyalty and I have mine, and only the almighty dollar came between us. I allowed a corruption into the heart of the city, and now it is my responsibility to expunge it.

Raul sits beside me, one of my African soldiers, short and gaunt. He follows my lead, pumping the vehicle full of lead with short bursts of automatic gunfire, but the road is not smooth enough for perfect shots, and so the beast persists. I wonder, how many bullets can a reinforced windshield really take before it cracks? Let's find out! The windshield is a broad target and I proceed to unload half a clip into the glass. Spots erupt like craters and Gavin speeds up. I can still see his eyes between the spiderweb cracks in the window.

"Hold on Monsieur Cinnamon," Raul says, and I grab the frame as the pursuing vehicle slams into us, rocking the Jeep and initiating a hazardous swerve. My driver struggles to straighten our trajectory, even as a body leans out the passenger side of the pursuing truck and takes pistol shots at me and my companions. I raise my gun to shoot back, but my aim is bad, damn wounded shoulder, and I lose more bullets in the dirt.

Time for a new clip, but I drop it as the armoured truck slams into us again. It's a heavier vehicle and we can neither outrun it nor withstand these beatings. Raul hands me a new clip and I tell him, "We have the advantage of a superior firing position! Lay it on him before he knocks us to shit!"

They are too close for us to shoot their tires, so we aim our bullets point-blank right into the glass. It can only handle so much damage. Soon it is a panel of white cracks, concave pane pushing inward and full of hot metal. Surely Gavin can barely drive like this. The roar of bullets drowns out the sounds of the engines, but not the loud crash as their truck smashes us again. This time we almost topple over, swerving left and right with a thrilling wobble. But after I load another clip and resume the barrage of bullets, I see that some metal is making it through and into their vehicle. My shoulder is almost numb now, and will be useless for days, but I must send Gavin to meet his brother lest I make the trip myself!

But as I spend another cartridge we turn a corner and I lose my aim. We are no longer surrounded by jungle, but instead travelling along a precarious road at the edge of a cliff. At the bottom of the rocky descent is a heavy river, and beyond that I discern towers of metal industrial equipment. The beacon has been leading us to an above-ground mine. But first we must safely descend this down-slope road, and avoid falling off the cliff.

The heavier truck turns the corner, and its engine roars as it speeds up to hurl its weight at us. We cannot afford to wobble on this narrow ridge. The obvious question seems to be whether we can shoot through that window before the truck slams into us, but in truth that still might not offer us salvation. What if I kill Gavin and his corpse-foot stays on the gas? Then we will all be doomed.

I grab a grenade from my belt and show it to Raul. He nods. We pull pins. Grenades hit the dirt like rocks and we cover our heads. The explosion rocks my body and shakes my truck. But the truck behind us has been more than shaken. It has been thrown directly in the air, wheels burnt off, shards of metal flying as the bulky machine spirals in space. Its forward momentum has not been thwarted, but instead diverted at an angle that takes it over the edge. The cliff is steep, so it takes a sickening long time for my enemy's capsule to find the ground, with a loud crashing smash and the crumpling of metal. Scraps of debris scatter like frightened mice. I can only imagine how the meat-bodies inside have been ravaged by the sudden impact. Their downward journey continues, tumbling and rolling until they finally find their place in the river. With a mighty splash they begin to sink. Birds take flight from a nearby tree.

The road takes us slowly to the bottom of the hill. The lush jungle we've left behind is replaced with a nation of mud. Bulldozers and excavator scoop-trucks prowl like dinosaurs in the distance. This devastated terrain is the ugly side of human innovation, where the ground has been ravaged for its minerals. We're driving into a scab upon the Earth, infested with towering steel frameworks which house drills, excavators, and processing mechanisms. Of course I have invested in such ventures, but they are still an ugly sight to behold. We pass a sign which proudly announces the name of the company which runs this show: Rasskakov Mining Co. My dear Felix Rasskakov, the bearded giant who was recently so curious about my project, owns this above-ground mine. Now I'm the curious one, wondering why the transmitter inside my nanobot canister is sending its signal from within the property of my business associate. At least I understand his curiosity now, since Agartha is a mere half-day's ride from here. This must be a new dig, since I took the time to make myself aware of all nearby excavations. If Felix has initiated this act of theft and murder, I'll gouge his eyes out and boil him in vinegar.

The dig sprawls out ahead of us and to the right, but the beacon sparkles to the left, near a village of trailers and small buildings. The administration and living area for the workers. I signal to the driver and he takes us in that direction. A single road travels through this village of mud and metal, and then disappears out into the jungle beyond headed to God knows where. We park in a parking lot beside trucks and Jeeps. As I prepare to get out, Raul turns his haunted eyes to me and says, "I fear a trap. We will not find our stolen goods here. We should leave this place, and you can find out who is behind the attack instead. Only then will you recover what is yours."

I pause to consider his words. Is it possible that they discovered the beacon inside the canister? If so they could indeed be laying a trap from which I may not have the manpower to escape. My phone tells me that the beacon is mere meters away, in the trailer across the muddy road. I shake my head. "You might be right, but you might be wrong. If the nanobots are in that trailer, we can retrieve them now. Who knows when they'll be so close again?"

But Raul insists. "You have created hope for my family, Monsieur Cinnamon. My brother and my son are both working and learning in Agartha, where your scientists teach us. After all the world has taken from Africa, you are giving something back. Do not risk it for this trap! You must escape and unmask our enemy, and leave us to do the fighting."

There is truth in his words. But the trailer, corrugated tin painted dirty yellow, is like a black box of mystery. What's inside? Is it my precious nanotech? Or men with guns? Maybe a bomb? As I ponder the dilemma, two white men in yellow hardhats approach. The taller one, with hard lines on his face and a strong frame, snaps at me in English with a thick Russian accent. "Who are you? Why these intrusions?" His tone leaves no doubt about his exasperation, but the gorilla-like gesticulations of his big hands adds a physical element to his challenge.

I stand tall and jump down from the truck. Standing before him, I don't quite reach his impressive height. "I am friends with your boss, Felix Rasskakov. You can call him right now. Tell him Julius Cinnamon has come to pick up the delivery."

The foreman's eyes narrow. I wonder if he has more to tell me, and whether I can get him to talk. But mostly I want him to get out of my way. Finally he nods. "I will call him right now. You stay here!"

"Of course," I smile as he points at the dirt. When he walks away, taking his friend with him, I turn to my men. "Okay, commandeer the construction equipment and tear this place apart like they tore apart Agartha."

Raul says, "What about the beacon? Will you go into the trailer?"

I spy an excavator with a double-scoop. "I have a better idea."

I stalk out of the village and into the realm of metal dinosaurs. The black man who drives the excavator puts his hands up when he sees my pistol. I'm sure Felix isn't paying the African natives enough to risk their lives. He jumps down and I take control of the track-driven monster. Now I'm towering over the little shacks and trailers. The tractor is too wide for the little road, so I nudge the shacks roughly out of the way. Snugly nestled in the road, I pull a lever to open the metal double-scoop. At first it is an awkward job to bring the clawed scoop down where I want it, but finally the metal teeth find the edge of the trailer. I laugh with delight at how easy it is to tear the end clean off the tiny building. It's like biting the end off a chocolate bar.

Now comes the tricky part! I move the truck forward some more and stretch out the craned neck so my scoop can grab the opposite end. There we have it. Just like the claw-crane game, I've grabbed the prize! The trailer is locked between the jaws of my scoop, and I lift it into the air. I dangle the building vertically, open end down, and I shake it back and forth. Furniture tumbles out. A desk and a couch, a table and chairs. Paper, knives, and coffee cups fall into the mud. Plus three men wearing grey uniforms, Alex's traitorous bastards, and I hope they broke their legs when they landed.

Sadly, they are hardly wounded. They try to run, so I bring the ragged edge of the trailer down on top of them, and I try to smush them like ants. I laugh at their screams as I unleash my monstrous vengeance, up and down, again and again. Now they are broken and bleeding in the mud and I toss the trailer aside and descend from my weaponized machine.

I have a pistol in my hand as I approach the ruined bodies of my enemies. Other buildings are being shoved aside and ripped open by the rest of the construction equipment, driven by my vengeful squad. The sounds of crunching and smashing is music to my ears. My eyes scan the scattered litter from the ruined trailer, seeking the shining metal of my nanobot canister, but I don't see it. One of the three men is dead, a crumpled mess of compound fractures, his head and torso smeared into the brown wet dirt of the road. A second man doesn't look much better, twitching, writhing and moaning, crumpled and twisted and crushed. With the sharp crack of a bullet I put him out of his misery. But a third man thinks he has the chance to escape. Frantically, he drags himself through the dirt toward another trailer. His legs are ruined, broken bones sticking out through ragged flesh. I shoot the dirt beside him and he turns around to face me.

The man opens one hand, and I see the blinking light of my beacon. "You looking for this?"

So Raul was right. "This was a trap after all," I say with a nod, levelling the pistol at his face. "Well it looks like I outsmarted you."

"Think twice, friend," A voice says behind me. I turn around and see another dirty, bloody figure standing before me. It is Gavin, and a crew of much cleaner-looking grey-suited soldiers.

"You survived your little tumble into the river," I say.

The hate in his eyes is multiplied by the dirt, water, and blood. He's like a swamp monster come for revenge from the netherworld. "How I would love to kill you right now," the Scotsman growls. "But poor dead old Alex's got a family to feed, and there's still money to be made. Now, you come back peaceful with us, and all this can still go according to plan. You won't get back what we've took from you, but you don't have to lose any more."

They're armed, and I'm standing here alone in the open road. I can't escape, and I can't beat them. I turn around, vaguely hoping my men may have gathered to turn this into a fight, but they're still in their trucks destroying the place. In fact, more grey-suited men have arrived, and I'm surrounded by enemies.

"Fuck," I say, and drop the pistol into the mud. For the first time, I see Gavin smile. Somebody has handcuffs, my worst fear, and he walks toward me.

From nowhere comes a great metal hook, swinging on a cable, to smash into the crew that confronts me. The hook knocks them down like bowling pins. I look up and see Raul driving the crane-truck from which my pendulum-saviour suspends. I take advantage of their momentary surprise, and chase after the arcing hook. I grab on just as it's lifting up into the air, pulling myself up to grab onto the cable for dear life. Below me, my pursuers open fire. But they miss their mark, and soon they are surrounded by other hostile construction equipment.

I fly through the sky, a human soap-on-a-rope, destined to cleanse the earth of the ugliness of my enemies. Raul was right. I should have skipped this obvious trap and escaped to the wider world where I could hunt those enemies with all my resources. Well now is my chance. Raul brings the hook over the top of a dump truck which is lumbering its load of dirt out of the mine. I let go and plummet into the loose gravel.

I stay low on the dirt so the drivers won't know I'm there, and I view the diminishing town behind me as we drive away into the jungle. My men are still destroying the town amid the sound of gunfire. They are outnumbered. There has been too much death already, and I hope they make it out alive. But I move away from this chaos so I can pursue a clearer path and reclaim Agartha for all who would bathe in her glory.

Chapter 7

The wind is rising, and waves come with it. Mother Nature is telling me to wait, but I have already waited days to get here. Days to think things through, to process the past and build a vision of the future.

Right now my only vision is the lightning flash which illuminates the layers of crumbling grey cliffs of my ancestral home. Frustrated waves smash against the jagged outcroppings at the steep base, and it is a hazardous climb to the top. I stand alone in an old fishing boat anchored a safe distance from the rocks, wearing tight swimming apparel and fanny packs full of dry climbing gear. I must scale these walls before the rain comes. I would have used the docks, but my dreadful father would not have let me past the gates.

The air is cold, but here the Adriatic sea is not frozen. I leap in like a seal and find myself immersed in the beautiful shock of frigid liquid.

These waters are my home but they will not hesitate to smash me against the stones. I aim for a slanted slab of grey as the waves toss me like a feather. I am a hornet in a hurricane. Pump my arms and kick my feet, I am equal to the faceless rage of nature! The constant rush, crash, and boom of the surging crests create a symphony of power not unlike my tumultuous heart. I am swimming in a friend! If she were to break my body on these stones, I would die in the embrace of the truest lover.

The biggest wave of all rises up behind me, pushing harder as it lifts me up in the air. Like a child on an amusement park ride I feel the excitement and fear until she brings me back down, on my feet, on the very slab that was my goal. I turn around to offer her thanks, and my Ocean Mother waves at me with a thousand frothing hands. More lightning lets me see my boat dancing like a demon to consecrate my journey.

Onward and upward. I hop from stone to stone until I am at the base of the cliff. This is a rock-climbers dream, with endless handholds and crevices. Geological time is laid bare in these layers of decaying firmament. How many tens of thousands of years have these layers been here, dutifully supporting the weight of the future? Continents have ancestors, too, buried beneath them. The elements have exposed them to me, and I will use them to climb up and achieve my destiny. I cannot even see the top.

A wave breaks behind me and sprays me with foam. The bottom layers are wet and must be met with care. A foot here, a hand there, and I am moving. Take no chances on these slippery ridges. Now I am sitting on a dry outcropping, above the reach of the waves and their dangerous moisture. Most of the climb is still far above me, and dark, but unless the rain starts soon I know I can make it. I shake the water out of my beard and replace my water-cap with a tuque from my pouch. Then I remove my gloves and dust my palms with chalk. The climb may begin in earnest. My wounded shoulder aches in anticipation of the work ahead, and I relish that ache.

My fingers find a hold and my muscles feast upon the challenge of pulling my weight heavenward. Here I come, Castle Blackburn. Here I come, dreadful father. I've heard your name too many times in these past days, just as my plans are being unravelled. Could it truly be that he has struck out to destroy the labour of his only son?

The rocks swell out above me. I must reach out and grab on, dangling where my feet can find no purchase. The lightning crashes and like a fool I look down to the hungry teeth of the sea below. They are eager to eat me up. Not today, cruel friends. I grunt and find a new chunk to grab. Pulling myself up, the chunk comes loose and tumbles into the air. My left hand slips and only three fingers of my right hand still grasp the hard rock and keep me from death. A single drop of rain finds those fingers, and I am only half way up. I dig my left hand into the hole where the chunk had come loose, and pull myself up some more. Hand over hand I climb over the swell, until finally my feet can find their own landings.

I grab another rock in the deepening dark, and the rock collapses in my hand. My fingers are immersed in thick goo, a viscous syrup. This was no rock, but instead a large egg among a cluster of spotted brown falcon eggs. I curse and wipe the murdered foetus on my chest. A winged shadow envelopes me. That's when I hear the shriek, and even above the force of the winds buffeting me I can feel the blast of air from the wings as a monstrous bird lands on my back, talons sinking into my shoulders. A hooked beak digs into my skull, and those massive wings beat once, twice, three times to pull me from my perch. I need my fists to fight, but I need my hands to hold onto the rocks! So I hold on tight with one hand and with the other I grasp the talon on my shoulder and try to break it. I roar as the talons only dig in deeper, and then the sky explodes with rain as my attacker digs into my head and rips at my flesh.

No good! I have a pick in my belt. It wasn't supposed to be a weapon, but it will certainly do! I aim up at the bird's head and swing until it hits squawking meat. The bird relents. Its wings flap like a dragon as it lets go and backs off. My foot slips in the rain and I stumble, but my hand-hold keeps me safe for now, and I find another place for my toes. Twisting my neck, I see the bird launching at me again. Lightning cracks the sky. Wide open wings envelope my world. She's freakishly huge, almost as tall as a man. Her beak is stone grey-blue, encased in a yellow cartilage. Maw gaping, sharp beak eager for my flesh, claws reaching out from the void. Those black hunters eyes. I think I'm in love!

I can't fight her on the cliff, so I leap out to meet her in mid-air. She falters and flaps. She didn't expect this, and my pickaxe sinks into her shoulder. "How do you like it?" I scream. She screams back, trying to keep altitude, but now we're spiralling together. I hold onto the pick, but she is no mountain and I'm pulling her down. Now I'm in a bad position. Her claw scrapes my face, barely missing my eye. With a great heaving lunge I twirl her around using only the pick, and wrap my other arm around her neck. I can let go of the weapon and straddle her back. She opens her wings to catch the wind. Instead of falling, now we are soaring.

But soaring is not enough. We're too heavy. "Fly, bitch!" I scream at her face. *She obeys.* She flaps those tremendous wings. Ever so slowly, pelted by a thunderous rain, we rise above the storming sea. I can feel her strength as she pumps her muscles. We are one. Her injured shoulder falters but does not fail. Finally we crest the top of the cliff and she swoops in to land. The two of us tumble together over the thin layer of grass and dirt upon the high rocks. I roll and land in a crouch. The pick is long gone, lost in the ocean, but I'm ready for a bare-knuckle battle with this magnificent beast. She spreads her wings and squawks with rage, but then turns and flies away. She got me away from her eggs. I peer over the edge and can barely see her halfway down, protecting her nest. She looks up at me with an angry eye, and I wave goodbye. I hope my father's greeting will be half as kind.

I turn around. The great bricks of Castle Blackburn stand before me. Looming spires and lightening sky define each other. The wind turns the rain into diagonal blades. I scale the stones, blessedly dry due to the angle of the rain, and climb in through my old window. Somehow it is colder inside than out, and a new kind of chill reaches deep into my bones. My darkened room is not as I remember it, though it has been decades since I visited. A layer of dust covers a bookshelf full of books I've never read. They are science-fiction and adventure stories: books about Martian colonies and medieval castles, where all I read was non-fiction history and science, even as a young boy. The desk is made of flimsier material than my old one, which was ancient heavy oak. I wonder who else has been using my room. But even the newer occupant has been gone long enough for dust to obscure every object. Or maybe my own memory is obscuring things. Maybe this was my room all along.

The rusty hinges crack and creak as I open the door into the hall. The noise will surely announce my presence, echoing throughout these catacomb-like passageways. It is almost pitch-black, but I've brought a pocket light. I can smell the dust. The spiral stairs are just where I remember and I make my way down. I don't know where my father will be, but I'll seek him out first in the main hall. It's an unnecessarily large cavern in this ridiculous monstrosity. Maybe our ancestors had held meetings or huge dinners there, but my father surely didn't.

Somehow I still remember the way. As I pass through another creaking door I finally find a lit hallway with its red carpets. He still uses flickering torches. The next door takes me into the main hall, as large as a small house, with its huge wooden table. I can't see the images in the tall stained glass windows, since no light seeks entry from the night sky. But I hear the howling wind and the heavy patter of the rain. I don't remember it being so dark.

"Hello, son," my father says, his voice a deep rich croak. He is not facing me but instead hunched over a large oak desk with his back to me, writing by hand on paper. There are stacks of paper on the desk and more on a nearby bookshelf which also holds leatherbound tomes. This massive room has become his office. A great elk's head hangs on the wall above him, in between faded tapestries. It all flickers in candle and torchlight.

"How did you know it was me?"

He turns around to look at me. His long hair is as black as ever, hanging like a waterfall. "Hello Julius," he says. Then turns back to his work. "Your face is ragged."

"And your face is withered and pale, and your back is hunched. But these injuries are nothing compared to the damage your minions caused to Agartha."

"What minions? Who is Agartha?"

"Don't act like you don't know. Agartha is the subterranean science-compound inside my

African volcano. And you robbed her."

"You bought a volcano? Selling cinnamon wasn't enough for you, then? Did you change your name to Volcano this time? Abandon another legacy?"

"A legacy of cinnamon is better than a legacy of rape," I growl, and my voice echoes throughout the chamber.

"What you call rape is what brought you into this world," he reminds me. He's still writing, probably just to show me that I'm not important enough for his full attention. "And I raised you nonetheless."

"I raised myself."

"You only finished raising yourself, after you ran away."

"After I found out what you had done to those nuns. A whole convent! Your personal brothel."

"There were many more," he says wistfully.

"How many of their sons did you raise?"

Now he finally stands and turns to face me. I had thought he would be as tall and imposing as I remembered, but he is old and weathered. A dark wooden cane helps him stand. I realize now that the desk on which he writes is my old one. I recognize the wood, and the pearl handles on the drawers. But his eyes still gleam as he snarls, "You could have been Count Maxwell Julius Blackburn the Second. The next Count Blackburn, with all my resources. You have my instincts, I can see it in you. But you threw it all away to be Julius Cinnamon, a spicy mockery of a proud lineage."

"The Blackburns haven't been counts for centuries. All you have is old money and old land. Everything I have I built for myself, and now you're trying to take it away. Why? Jealousy? To teach me a lesson? Or did you steal my battery so this old cave can finally experience electricity?"

The old man chuckles and gestures at the desk behind him. "I am writing my memoirs before I die. Whatever plans you have, they would only make the story more interesting. Why would I attack you? I hardly think about you. When I found out you changed your name, and made your fortune selling cinnamon, I lost interest. What makes you think it was me? Or did you come here secretly looking for my help?"

"I don't need help. I keep hearing your name from people who are too curious about my business."

"You fool," he says. "They're using my name as a decoy. While you're here blaming your father for your troubles, their trail grows cold. Maybe you don't have my instincts after all."

"But how did they even learn the name Blackburn if not from you?"

"You may have kept your ancestry a secret, but the rest of the world didn't. I don't know how they found out, but it wasn't from me. You've come to the wrong place."

To my surprise, I believe him. I stand in confusion as he turns back to his memoirs, writing as if I'm not even here. I thought I was following the ultimate clue, and headed straight for the source. But now I'm empty-handed. I hate him even more, and in my heart I recognize a desire to be able to blame him for all this. It would be satisfying to thwart him once again, and take back what was mine. But I have no choice but to slink out of my father's castle and follow other leads. As I exit the room he doesn't even say goodbye.

I will at least use the front door this time. The way out takes me through the chamber of statues. Torchlight casts shadows across the features of stone sculptures of my ancient forebears. Stern, ugly faces. Many wear beards, and I swear I can recognize myself in those eyes. At the far end are two suits of armour standing guard, holding spears at an angle. Above the entry is a broadsword, wielded once by Charles Blackwell and his sons and grandsons. The sheath is ugly cracked leather, but the hilt is exquisite. I decide to salvage something from this awful visit, and I climb the rough-hewn stones of the door-frame. With one foot on the head of the suit of armour I lift the heirloom-weapon from its mount and leap to the ground. The cross-guard is carved to resemble falcon wings. The leather grip is dry but tight. The pommel is a disk with the letter B engraved in medieval script. I pull the blade slightly from the sheath. Instead of dull rusted metal I see torchlight reflected in the smooth steel surface. This is a work of art. When I find whoever has invaded Agartha, I will end their lives with this piece of history. I can skip the crimes of my father and still inherit something of the dignity of my ancient lineage.

I rest the blade on my shoulder and exit the room, but something suddenly blocks my path. It is a spear. The suit of armour is animated! He pushes me back with his wooden stick, and holds out his metal hand for the sword I have stolen.

"Who the fuck are you?" I demand. He offers no answer. Well, he may be heavy and strong but he can't move as fast as me in that oppressive gear. I knock the spear aside and dodge for the exit. But the second guard catches me and grabs my shoulder in his hard hands. His squeeze is terrible and digs into the falcon wound. As I try to twist free the original spear-holder grabs the sword from my shoulder and tosses it back across the room where the beautiful artifact clatters roughly on the floor. I give up on the sword now and aim only for escape, but these rough men have me. No kick or jab can wound them, and no wrestling or wriggling can help me escape their steel embrace. They lift me up, carry me to a window, and toss me out onto the wet grass where the wind and rain tease my wounds. I am denied answers, denied the beautiful broadsword, and even denied a dignified exit.

Somewhere in the distance the rumble of thunder is pierced by a falcon's cry.

Chapter 8

A hotel room in Slovenia gives me a place to think, and a place to drink. A man needs momentum in his thoughts and in his behaviour, but mine has been dashed against the rocks. There are those who draw strength from their families, but my visit home has delivered an unexpected dose of poison to my soul at a time when I am most vulnerable. When I need strength the most is when it has been most heartily ripped away. I need a woman, and I need a plan.

I hit the bottle hard, both down at the bar with Scotch, vodka, and cognac, and up in my room with more of the same. The booze kills the delicious pain in my heavily-stitched face, where the falcon's talons will leave a handsome scar. But they also kill the unfocused rage that comes from nowhere, inspired for unknown reasons by the soul-scattering confrontation with my ugly ancestry.

I take a cleaning lady to bed after some drunken wooing. She is half my age but twice my equal in carnal gumption. I bury my face in the dark and tangled forest between her smooth thighs, and I bury my masculine monolith in every tunnel that she allows. Her body becomes a surging continent of hot joy, her breasts two Agarthas reclaimed by my greedy hands.

There is a fine line between lust and rage. The animal energy I must embrace lest it consume and destroy me. Gripping and pounding my rage into her sweetness in a vicious act of alchemy which transmutes the hate into a blinding joy, I push her beyond the brink. She breaks her fingernails in the bedsheets as she claws herself away, and in my back as she pulls me closer. I utterly ruin her and she loves me for it. Her shuddering voice teases me out of my sourness. The oblivion of orgasm reawakens my conquered beast, but the delicate beauty of her femininity reminds me of my own gentleness.

Together we stand on the balcony, naked in the cold and drinking vodka as we look out upon the snow-covered roofs. She has returned off-duty so I can ravage her properly. I find it's easier to think with this lovely woman beside me. Should I hunt down big bearded Felix Rasskakov, since his company provided the location for my ambush? Should I put old Viktor Sabitov to the question for his misleading utterance of my awful family's name? I still want to go straight to the source, the mastermind, and cut the beast off at the head. But it may be more wise to pace myself, tease out the details, and form a clearer picture. I bend my lady over the stone rail of the balcony and fuck her for the whole city to see. With my drink in one hand and her hip in the other, my mind is filled with the answer. Jasserty Holdings, the name on both contracts which different men risked their lives to coerce me to sign. Through that name I will find my stolen goods and the devious mastermind who has orchestrated this plot. A smile returns to my face as I remember that this is a game, and win or lose I am enjoying it. The meeting with my father had made me forget that. The wrong emotions are sometimes wrapped up in family.

Back in the hotel room my maid wraps herself around me like a spider, like a cobra. She pins me in place and uses me to bring herself to heaven, over and over again. I only release my milk over her body, or inside her womb, when she finally allows it. But she allows it many times before she finally leaves me to a satisfied sleep.

In the morning after a shower and a huge

breakfast I spend hours researching Jasserty Holdings. The internet gives no sustenance to my curiosity, and my telephone calls and personal appeals to knowledgeable colleagues also turn up nothing. No business listing divulges any relevant info. A man of my means should be able to solve this puzzle quickly enough, but there are thousands of businesses in every nation and I don't even know which continent is harbouring this wretched cabal.

Puzzling over a light lunch and a beer in the hotel restaurant, a switch finally clicks in my brain and I realize that I've seen that name before. I pull out my wallet where I still have stashed the business cards that I stole from that unlucky spy, Rusty Knight. Among the cards is the Spanish salvage company, Jasserty Salvage. Can it be the same Jasserty as in Jasserty Holdings? Phone number and address are written in blue ink on the thick brown paper, gifts from the gods. I finish my meal and prepare to travel again.

And so I find myself on the docks in a Spanish port town looking out at the turquoise waters of the Mediterranean sea. The wooden planks echo the footsteps of busy sea-goers returning from or heading to their vessels. In the distance a cargo ship heads to an industrial harbour, but closer at hand are sailboats and various forms of pleasurecraft. Another section of this expansive marina showcases heavily-equipped research vessels. I wonder which ones belong to Jasserty Salvage.

I pass offices and storehouses, shops and restaurants, until I find the winning address. It is a stone building among several identical units right on the boardwalk. A humble sign hangs above the door, stating the name of the company without fanfare. I blend in perfectly with my khakis and tackle vest, where I've stashed handcuffs and knives along with lock-picking equipment if necessary. I am grim and cheerful. This is a game, and yet it is more. My daughter is certainly independent and self-sufficient, but I want her to be able to draw on my resources to pursue her ambitions. I don't intend to hand her a ruined empire. I intend to elevate her species through the secret workings of Agartha.

The door jingles as I enter. To my right is a waiting area with chairs and a coffee table. On my left is an office area where a man sits surrounded by papers, tapping on a computer keyboard. Beyond I see rows of shelves, scantily occupied by small wooden crates. The largest ones in the back are barely the size of an oven. I had held some hope that I might easily find the massive battery here, but that thing would take up half of this entire building.

"Can I help you?" the slight man asks me from his desk. He has pitch-black hair slicked back over his skull and I swear to God I recognize those eyes. Black pants and a light brown shirt. I notice he's no longer surrounded by papers. He has stashed them away somewhere. Suspicious, or just prudently neat?

"I'm here to file a complaint," I say. "Something of mine has been illegitimately salvaged."

The man smiles silently and leans back with arrogant comfort. He looks me up and down. "Are you the 18th century Spanish pirate, Diego Gonzales?"

"Maybe."

"We brought up a crate of Scotch from your sunken ship, with four bottles sealed and intact. If you want them back you'll have to prove your identity. Hey, did your parrot give you that nasty scratch?"

He's talking about the stitches on my face. "Close enough. What else have you dug up in the past few weeks?"

His eyes move to the rows of crated goods. "I don't share my bosses' inventory with strangers. Please, give me some details. What are you looking for, that you think we've improperly salvaged?"

"Nanobots," I say. "And a battery. Not to

mention the lives of my scientists. All stolen from my African volcano laboratory."

"Our boats don't work very well in volcanoes."

"Either do your helicopters," I say. "Their success rate is one out of three."

His frown is deep and his smooth features wrinkle in seriousness. "Okaay... you know, we go out in the sea and look for sunken ships, usually ones that are very old. We really don't have anything like nanobots and batteries. I'm clearly missing something here. Care to fill me in?"

"Do you go out personally to dig up these ships?"

He gestures at his neat desk and computer. "I do the paperwork and inventory. I'm basically an accountant."

"Let me see your inventory list."

He shakes his head.

"Is your boss in today?"

"Mr. Jasserty doesn't spend much time here, and the rest of the team are out to sea."

I offer a casual shrug. "What harm would it do to let me look at your inventory? Nobody has to find out. It will put my mind at ease."

"That's valuable information. We sell our stuff at auctions, and sometimes privately. My answer is a definitive *no*. I could take your name and phone number and pass it on to Mr. Jasserty. Otherwise I have to ask you to leave."

"I'm not leaving until I look at that list."

"You don't have a choice."

Handcuffs dangle from my hand. "I think I do."

"Kinky," he says, casually pulling open a drawer. I leap into action. Before I reach him he has already palmed a snub-nosed pistol. He doesn't get the chance to aim it before I grab his wrist and twist. He grunts and drops the weapon on the desk, punching my ribs with his other fist. I smack him harder than he's ever been smacked and he falls off the chair onto the hard tiles, dazed. Seconds later I've got him face-down on the floor and I cuff his hands behind his back. His wallet is in his back pocket and I take it.

"You shouldn't sit on your wallet," I advise him. "It's bad for your back." I pull out his identification. He is Samuel Saffron, from the USA.

"I shouldn't sleep face-down either," he mutters into the dirt.

"Try to stay awake then, Mr. Saffron. Where is that name from, anyway?"

"My Dad."

Snarky fucker. I laugh and haul him up to sit against a nearby shelf. Then I sit in his chair and look for the papers he had so diligently hidden when I arrived. I find them in a manilla folder on the floor, wedged between the desk and a filing cabinet. There are gridded maps with specific locations marked and labelled, including their latitude and longitude coordinates. A few stapled documents seem to be proposals for future salvage expeditions.

Folded in half is a list of incoming inventory complete with dates, sources, and destinations. Swivelling around to face young Samuel I say, "These names are cryptic. Can you help me decipher them?"

"No," he says.

I proceed anyway. "Gonzales Scotch and Mountain Spice came in today, from two different sources. What is Mountain Spice?"

"A defunct spice company."

"A couple days ago you received Rock Eater and Bethika Battery, salvaged from Metpo. This seems oddly familiar, do you know what those are?"

He shakes his head. "That shipment didn't come here. Can't you even read the sheet you stole?"

He's right. They went to a warehouse in Algiers and then onto new destinations. Rock Eater is obviously the nanobots, and Bethika Battery is my beloved ultimate battery. Metpo looks like the Russian word for underground, so it may be a pseudonym for Agartha.

An odd listing catches my eye. "A thousand barrels of... anti-mag?"

"Re-routed somewhere else. No room here."

I have all I need, but I want more. I look at the listing for the Scotch. It's my lucky day. It's right here in the warehouse. Their labelling system makes it easy to find the right crate on the shelf, shoulder height. I take it down and set it on the desk. With a crowbar I pry open the wood, nails screeching and bending. They've packed the four old bottles in foam. I remove two and appraise them. The bulbous bottles look new, filled to the cork with no evaporation. The corks are safe under thick blobs of wax. The brown liquid has a mystical hue as the light shines in through the window.

"Two hundred year old Scotch," I marvel.

"It doesn't age in the bottle," Samuel reminds me.

"But I'll be drinking history."

I turn to leave with my treasures, but Samuel complains again. "Will you at least leave me the key so I can get out of these handcuffs?"

I consider his proposal, then shrug. Setting the bottles down, I climb up one of the shelves and place the key on a crate at the very top.

"Are you fucking serious?"

The door-chimes share my laughter as I exit.

Chapter 9

I have already cased the joint, and I'm ready for a midnight assault. I'm not experienced at breaking and entering but this warehouse appears to have minimal security. They have one night guy who stays in an upstairs office plus a patrolman doing rounds among the many buildings in this industrial park. There are probably cameras inside but I hope my identity is obscured by this ski mask. I have rope, knives, lock-picks, and a variety of items which may help me in this clandestine endeavour. I am a spider. Success means sneaking in unnoticed, grabbing the nanobots off the shelf, and dissolving into the night.

I am wedged in between a giant dumpster and the corrugated steel of the factory next-door to the warehouse. The light is on upstairs in the security office. His window is open to permit a breeze which offers respite from the heat of the American south. More importantly he has just left the room, perhaps to go to the bathroom. I know this because I have already scaled the wall to plant a tiny camera in the corner, providing a feed which I watch on my phone. It's frustrating that I haven't seen his face, so I can't properly judge my opposition, but if my plan works I won't be facing him at all. All is quiet and I prepare to run until I hear the footsteps of the outside patrolman. He clomps casually past my hiding spot, uncomfortably close, but he does not notice my black visage among the shadows. When he's gone around the corner I pace silently over the parking lot until I am beneath the yellow window. A ground-level window-ledge allows me to reach a short section of pipe from which I can grab the security window. The riskiest part of this adventure is that I have to cut the screen out so I can climb in. My knife slits the bottom and both sides, creating a flap, and then I stand inside the florescent radiation of the security office.

The ledger I stole in Spain tells me the address where the canister has been delivered, but not where the warehouse has stored it internally. Luckily, while observing their operations during the daytime I saw that they keep an updated inventory list at a desk down on the main floor beside the big bay doors. So I pass quickly through this little office and into the hallway. The bathroom is clearly labelled on the right so I go left and open a door which lets me out onto a catwalk which overlooks the rows and rows of heavy metal shelves, two stories high. During my research I had found out that Sunderwich University is the major client for this storehouse. I wonder what kinds of expensive research equipment and museum-worthy artifacts are gently stored in the wooden crates which fill the shelves. Some of the crates are massive, including two which just sit on the floor because they're simply too large for the shelves. I would love to steal everything in this place, but I will settle for simply retrieving that which is mine.

After a quick scan to double check that nobody is around I pad down the metal stairs and make my way to the cement wall. Dim lights hang between the aisles and I slither around their penetrating radiance. I am at the desk. It stands before me bathed in holy light, and the inventory list rests casually on the top. Nobody is around and I could just take it without being seen, but as a matter of principle I don't want to appear on any cameras if I can avoid it. So I hit the ground and roll under the desk. From this vantage point I can see up the aisle to the catwalk where I so recently stood. To my surprise the security man is there, gazing out at his domain. I stay still, aware that I am somewhat visible in the dim light. But the lightly-bearded, chubby man turns around and heads back to his office where he can sit and get chubbier. Something tingles in my brain. Do I recognize this man?

My hand snakes out and grabs the papers from atop the desk. Then I roll back into the darkness and pull out my phone to shine a light on the list. The Rock Eaters arrived just ahead of two Eight-Legged Guards, whatever those are.

My treasure is in the large centre aisle, on the second shelf down from the top. That aisle is unfortunately the most visible, but the shelves themselves are immersed in murk. As I climb the appropriate unit I feel the darkness as a living thing, a throbbing organism which hides me in its sanctuary and gives me strength. The shelves are tall enough that I can sit when I reach the right level. A latched wooden box sits on my right, and a nailed-shut wooden crate extends in a long rectangle to my left. I have a multi-tool pocket knife which I use to break the latch on the box. When I open the hinge I see my precious canister nestled snugly in a bed of foam beads. Victory at last!

Curiosity makes me linger. With my knife I wedge open the lid of the rectangular box on my opposite side. Every little noise seems to echo immensely, so I wiggle and push ever so softly. I am hoping to see some advanced telescope or lightweight technology that I can easily steal. I've developed sticky fingers after taking the Scotch from Mr. Saffron at Jasserty Salvage. What I find instead are several rusted old swords, warped like arthritic fingers, resting in shredded plastic. They might have some historic importance, but they are ugly as sin and certainly useless as weapons. I place the lid back down.

I am reaching for my canister when all the lights erupt in horrible brightness, blinding me momentarily. An unexpected voice cuts through the unexpected radiance, blasting its announcement from every speaker.

"Julius!" The man's voice proclaims. "You've come for your goodies! Except they were never yours, were they? But they were never mine, either. That's why I've got to give them back to the university. Now that they're on the books they were never really stolen, right? Just misplaced. And I can still get paid for killing you! They'd pay me more to capture you alive, but that's too dangerous."

"Blake!" I scream, remembering how he killed my men and wiped shit on my face. I can't climb down yet. My eyes haven't adjusted to the light. "Come and fight me then! Now's your chance you fat traitor!"

He laughs. "I'm not that fat, but I'm fat enough to lose if we fought. I'm going to let my two eight-legged guards do the fighting!"

Below me I vaguely see the two gigantic crates, too large to fit on the shelves. There's one on each end of this main aisle. Lights suddenly blink upon their top corners. Electronic latches?

The inward-facing sides of the boxes open down like doors, and just as my vision finally adjusts I see two gigantic spiders crawl tentatively out of their wooden prisons. Their spider-bodies are as large as gorillas, and those legs- my God, they're *huge!* One has black skin which shines smoothly with only a thin layer of spiky hairs. The other is brown, thicker and hairier. And they each have eight bulbous alien eyes above chalicerae longer than human arms, like mandibles which cover the mouth, ending in sharp glistening claws. They have two eyes on the top of their head, two giant ones in front, and a curving row of four small ones just below. They can see all around, and they see me right away.

"They've been here a few days," Blake announces apologetically. "And they're probably hungry. Lucky for me they already have a taste for human flesh!"

They move slowly and awkwardly at first, perhaps also disoriented by the florescent onslaught. Their two front legs reach up into the air and test the ground like someone stumbling in the dark. But they are heading for me without a doubt. I can't climb down amongst them but I'm not safe up here either. Even as my mind considers escape routes the black spider appears below me and the other has already climbed halfway up the shelves. Long legs reach up at me from below like a child reaching for its father, but those mandibles have sharp claws, and when they open up they reveal a hungry anus-like mouth, gaping for sustenance.

I reach into the crate full of rusty swords and wield one of the imperfect weapons. One hand gripping the rail and my feet planted on the shelf, I lean over the arachnid and hurl the historic instrument into that disgusting orifice with all the might I can muster. The sword does a quick spin before the dull blade lodges itself perfectly in the spider's mouth, protruding like a flag pole. Eight legs scramble in a frenzy as it backs away, smashing into the opposite shelving unit and causing the whole works to rattle. It rears up on its hind legs and uses its forelegs to try to tease out the offending splinter of steel.

No time to rest. The brown spider is upon me, ready to engage in a vertical battle. These shelves have no back, so I can slip through to the other side. I grab the box that holds the nanobots and a fresh sword, sliding past two more boxes. I have to drop them both on the floor so I can free my hands and begin to climb down. The spider also fits, but it's a tight squeeze and I'm down on the opposite floor before he's through. Stealth is no longer an option, so I just want to get my nanobots and find an emergency exit.

Now the black spider is coming at me, mouth bleeding and front-arms flailing. It has removed the sword from its mouth, and it towers above me like a waterfall of horror. I barely have time to scoop up the sword, batting at its limbs as they seek to grab me. I forget the nanobots for now. My life is more important, though barely. The spider is faster than me, and though I strike hearty blows I fear I may get tired before they do. How can I get past those legs and damage the body?

The brown spider descends upon me and I take a swing at one striking limb. This is a losing battle, so I dodge into the shelves again, in between two large boxes where the opening is too thin for them to follow. I can hear the skittering feet as one of the monsters scrambles around the shelves to find me on the other side. I can see the shadow of the other, who is climbing directly over the top. When the black one peeks its ugly head around the far corner, I hurl my sword like a throwing axe, smacking the great eyes and causing it to scramble again. I dodge back through the way I came, intending to grab my nanobots and make for an exit, but the brown spider has merely waited on the other side. Big wooly arms take hold of my body. It's almost gentle as it lifts me up towards the stabbing claw-arms in front of its mouth. I wrestle to be free but three arms keep moving, rolling me up toward its face.

In my panic to escape I've forgotten that I'm already armed. Knives appear in my hands. One flies through the air and sticks in the spiders' eye. The other I use to hack and slash at the grabbing legs that manhandle me. The spider drops me and I tumble to the hard cement. The black spider is back around again and coming at me, but one of its eyes is now deflated and oozing dark-red pus. I climb the next row of shelves, back up to where the other swords await. I grab another weapon from its bed and shove the others down onto the cement with a sharp smash and clatter. Now I head up to the very top level where I can hide between two large boxes, and hurriedly unfasten the loop of rope strapped to my back. I tie one end around the pole that holds up the shelves, and the other end into a wide lasso.

I am surrounded. The brown spider reaches in from the main aisle, and the black one stares at me through the opposite opening. The brown one is larger and a little slower, so I rush him with sword and rope. With the metal I bat aside his reaching leg and jab the rusted blade into his eye. I shove with all my might. A chittering sucking sound. He reaches out with two legs to grab me, and I deftly pull the lasso over those limbs.

Beneath his body I run, past the clamping claws above its mouth, pulling at the rope to tighten it around his two foremost legs. I try climbing down, but he has so many legs! They grab me again, and I am caught. They move too fast for me to fight, and I'm amazed at how dexterous these beasts can be.

Once again I am inches from its mouth, meeting an alien monster face to face. For a wondrous moment I merely stare in awe at the face of this killing machine. He almost deserves his victory. I wonder how I look to him. Is he impressed at my ingenuity? Do any thoughts take place behind those alien eyes?

Well he's not a fast learner. I deliver another blade into yet another of his vulnerable eyes, and I grab the sword that still protrudes from his face. Razor-sharp pincers snap together inches from my neck and I almost piss myself, flinching and stretching. When I pull out the sword a hunk of gore comes with it, and then I bring the thing back down in an arc to smash my opponent on his head with a mighty thunk.

I am dropped again, this time from a greater height. The two-storey fall would wound me, so I grab the rope connecting spider to shelf and swing, dangling and letting myself down more slowly. And then I run, because the black spider is coming around the other corner. I run across the centre aisle and to the wall, to hide behind the opposite row of shelves and stand with my sword at the ready.

The brown one is nearly half-blind, but he races after me until the rope stops him. He makes it just past this widest aisle. The lasso is tight over his whole head. I've got him trapped and now I just need to stay out of his reach and deal with the black spider. I still have this sword, but sadly I am out of knives.

What is this? The bound brown spider is still moving closer! He grabs the shelf in front of me and continues to pull. Will he tear his own head off in his struggle? Instead I see that he's pulling down the shelf to which he's tied! This can only be good. I tease him forward, wondering what kinds of behaviour I can exhibit to make myself appear more delicious and enticing.

I feel like his coach. "Come on, spider! You can do it!"

He reaches and pulls, and makes it past the next aisle. That's when the massive shelf crosses the tipping point and begins to fall under its own weight. Now I have to run, since the falling shelf will give the brown spider some slack. The crash is deafening and actually hurts my ears with its sharp BOOM. I didn't run away fast enough, and now the spider has hold of my leg. But a hard swing with the blunt blade cracks a leg and it scurries back.

Now I'm hunting for the black spider, pacing slowly through the aisles and trying to listen to its scurrying feet. My nemesis doesn't show his face. Has he given up? I come out into the main aisle from the other end now, and see the shelving unit, now horizontal on top of a pile of ruined boxes. I wonder how many thousands of dollars worth of equipment have been destroyed. All I can see are the splinters of the boxes that held them.

But I also see black spider legs twitching amongst the rubble. The poor fellow was crushed when the wall came down. I walk atop the fallen shelving until I am standing above him, then I reach down and pull the throwing knife from his eye. The brown spider eyes me from afar, but makes no move to attack again. I grab my canister of nanobots and proceed back up the stairs to find Blake.

Is he waiting with a gun to blow my brains out? If so he will only have one shot before I put this bloody throwing knife into his eye. Instead I find him straddling the window sill, not athletic enough to climb down and too frightened to jump.

"Where the fuck did you get two giant spiders?" I ask him.

Despite his indecisive position he speaks with a confidence which is supposed to be menacing. "The people who want you are very powerful," he tells me. "They can get anything."

"And I can kill anything," I respond, rummaging through his desk for duct tape.

When I reach for him he finally gets the nerve to jump. I have to grab his leg and haul him awkwardly back in through the window. I bind his hands, feet, and mouth. "I would let you live," I whisper in his ear, "but you murdered Wallace."

He doesn't realize what's really happening until I drag him through the door. His muffled screaming diminishes into despairing wails when I bang his head on every step coming down the stairs. I toss him like a wriggling slug so he's within reach of the brown spider. "A peace offering," I tell the spider, who moves tentatively forward for its meal.

As I turn to leave I notice a sparkle amongst the splinters of ruined crates. First I think it is shattered glass, but on closer inspection I see that it is diamonds! I literally drool. There must have been an entire crate of them stashed here, and now they're exposed. Well I can't take them all, but I'm happy enough to take a pocketful. Maybe two pocketfuls plus a handful in my pouch. You can never be too rich. And it's all for the cause! Then it's up the stairs and out the window to disappear into the darkness.

This wasn't a perfect success, since I wasn't as sneaky as I had planned. But it was a good night, and bodes well for the future.

Chapter 10

The deep grey-blue clouds are withered ghosts haunting the night sky. The sound of the undead ocean disturbs any hope for peace, with its thousand tiny waves frothing over each other and lapping up the shore and the docks like an army of liquid skeletons grasping for the lifeforce of the living.

Again I wait in the shadows. Again my plan includes a level of stealth which may prove unrealistic. What is different is that tonight I am better prepared for a full-on assault. Along with my knives I've brought a pistol, some dynamite, and I have a crew waiting nearby with a helicopter. When I find my truant battery I can call in the cavalry to carry her away from her captors. I have put the nanobots in a safe deposit box along with my stolen Scotch and the diamonds. If I can only get this battery to a safe location then I can turn my full attention to the ongoing siege at Agartha.

My tormentors will certainly be aware of my recent arachnoid catastrophe, so surely they will have set some sort of trap. But I spent two days observing this lone wooden warehouse on the southern coast of Texas and have seen no signs of any security or obvious danger. It should be easy for me to sneak in and behold my stolen cargo, and this makes me suspicious.

Another thing bothers me. My Spanish inventory list does not actually indicate this address as the delivery location for the so-called Bethika Battery. Instead it lists geographic longitude and latitude which puts it a half-kilometre off the coast. When I gaze out at the ocean I see nothing. So I'm operating under the assumption that some kind of vessel received my battery at those coordinates, and then brought them here to this address, which is conveniently owned by Jasserty Salvage.

The wind is crisp. The water is louder than my feet upon the wooden planks of the dock as I approach the flake-painted walls of my destination. A boat tied to the dock bobs up and down. I peer through a window and see only vague shapes in the darkness. I have a microphone, and my helicopter crew hears everything I do. When shit goes down, help will already be on its way.

The door is locked with a mere padlock. Embarrassing. I break it with a mini bolt cutter. I have a pistol in my hand as I pour myself silently through the door. Once inside it's easier to see, and what I see is that my battery is not here. The huge room is almost empty, save for some diving gear and an empty desk. Hanging on the back wall I see a surprising number of what appear to be heavy-duty scuba tanks, and a few normal-sized air tanks in the corner.

"There's nothing here," I tell my helicopter man.

He responds in my ear. "Are you coming back, then?"

"No," I tell him. I look at the diving gear and find an air tank which is full with air. "I'm going to check out the precise coordinates."

Within minutes I'm out on the open water. The little motor boat was tied up, not even locked, with a half a tank of gas. The motor hums with the joy of its own exertion, doing what it was built to do. My phone's GPS will tell me when I reach the sweet spot. Of course the thought has crossed my mind that the diving gear and the boat are a little too convenient, and I am walking into exactly the trap that I anticipated. But the ocean is clear and calm all around. This is no trap, unless someone is waiting for me underwater. I expect I'm pursuing a dead lead. The battery is long-gone and I'll have to come back at this from another angle. But I can't leave until I visit the location, both above and below the water's surface.

I stop the boat and prepare myself for descent. The pistol and explosives will stay up here. All I need is the big waterproof flashlight. But I strap two knives to my ankles, just in case. Then it's backwards over the edge to splash into the water. I sink beneath the cool waves.

I am a fish now. A fish-man seeking his underwater Valhalla. My distant ancestors ventured to crawl onto the land, and now I return to their world. A pilgrimage. The only light comes from my two-handed rig, the massive bulb creating a headlight cyclops. It is raining bubbles and particles. I cast the light downward, and down I swim. I'm a proficient diver but no expert, and I've never gone under alone or at night. The sea is full of monsters and I wonder how far away the closest ones are. I can't see them, but can they sense me? Hello ancient cousins. Do they know that we're related? I was once one of them. We recognize ourselves in the apes, but even a fish has a face.

Something long and evil wriggles past the most distant reach of my vague beam. An eel? A giant snake? My helicopter pilot can't save me down here.

A shape emerges. A long bar stretches across my field of vision. I would guess that it's a metal bar crusted with ocean growth, lingering film like a dusty spiderweb. More than a bar now, this is the railing on the deck of a ship! I can't see the whole vessel since my vision is limited to this ray of light, but I can see the platform, the hull, and the entrance that leads into the dark interior of the ship. It has landed upright, at a slight angle. I resist the urge to go inside, and instead I stop my descent and cast the light around for evidence of the battery. The ocean floor is a sandy plateau. Barely a rock or fish breaks the monotony. I decide to take a look around the area, using the drowned boat as a reference point. As I travel around the ship I discover more dirt. A cluster of seaweed pokes out from behind a boulder. Some growth, like flowers with no stems, living origami unfolding in the ocean currents, makes its home along the ship's hull. Further down I spy a school of flat-bodied fish pouring out of a great rupture in the side of the ship, taking no notice of me. The light flashes off their scales and their eyes, a sharp contrast from the brown and blue darkness all around. But my stolen treasure does not present itself.

Around the other side of the ship the ground descends in a hill down to God-knows-what. Now that I'm down here I want to explore forever. I want to go down that hill and find a secret cave, fight a shark and die where I belong. Or maybe I'll find a mermaid and live happily ever after. Instead, I decide to abandon this stupid expedition and return to the surface where I can follow real evidence.

But something has caught my eye. When I turn my light away from the downhill slope, light remains. Are my eyes playing tricks on me? Is the pressure doing something to my brain? I'm sure I see something glowing, deep down the hill.

I head for the light. The slope quickly steepens and I fly straight on like a bird, watching the ground drop away beneath me into darkness. I consider going down and following the slope, but now something looms before me. Great shadows rising up from below, towers of crooked darkness like inverted submarine nebulae. The green waters are lit up by large orbs resting on the ocean floor. Amid all the spooky light, with its flashing fish-shadows and dancing debris of dirt and decay, is the vague shape of this centrepiece of darkness. Like a great black spiked rock, a castle-sized sea-urchin, a rock-monster reaching up to the surface. But on top of it, I see a red cube. All I really see are its glowing veins, the organic neural net of my Ultimate Battery living the life aquatic these days. The veins stand out against the darkness on top of the big black monstrosity, just at the base of its spires which reach up like arthritic tentacles.

Is my battery powering those glowing orbs? What is this massive altar on which my battery rests?

I swim down. I must touch it. I can't leave until I'm absolutely sure. I pass between the spires, still unsure whether they are rock or some life-form. Now I am on top of it, and the Ultimate Battery is unmistakable. Under the glow of my flashlight it is easier to see the textured surface between the intricate organic network embedded in the metal. The black material absorbs most of the light, but the faint organic grid reflects it and even seems bio-luminescent. I put one palm flat on her surface. I cannot speak with the breathing apparatus in my mouth, so I give her a silent promise that I will return. A crab crawls across the top and looks up at me, staring with his buggy little eyes. He waves his claws like he's saying hello, or he's trying to warn me of something. This is my most peaceful moment. I belong underwater with this crustacean comrade atop my Ultimate Battery, renamed Bethika by her kidnappers. Her slave name. All I can hear is my own breath, and the crushing weight of the ocean.

A net appears. It casts no shadow as it rains down from above, since all the light is from below. My crab was indeed trying to warn me, and now he's scurrying away. I reach for the edge, seeking to get out from under it before it closes, but my unseen attacker is deft and nimble and I feel the rope grid tighten around me. I'm already being pulled up, and hard. My hands poke out between the holes and I grab a knife to saw at my constraints. But now my attacker shows himself, grabs my wrist and attempts to disarm me. Not an easy task. With my other hand I grab my other knife and put it in his belly. Rip him open. My flashlight shines up from below, illuminating his intestines as they spread out into the lonely water. Sad man, he's trying to put them back in. They look like ocean flora. His guts belong here. He can be a gift to my crab friend, who tried to warn me.

Now I'm sawing at the ropes as a force pulls me up. Great catch today, one murderous billionaire. I cut a hole wide enough to escape, but I must still disentangle my arms and legs. Right arm, then left. Now my head is through. The rope continues its ascent and I dangle behind, flipper-feet caught in the webbing. It's too awkward for me to reach up and get free.

I break the surface. Lights flash in my eyes and I can't see who it is that grabs me. I slash out with a knife and somebody screams, but then I'm face-down on the deck of whatever boat I've been pulled onto with somebody's knees on my back. A knife-blade presses against the rubber suit that covers my throat. "We want you alive," a man tells me, "but we kind of want to kill you, too."

They haul me to my feet. I'm standing on the deck of a small trawler yacht, surrounded by armed men. Three are bald and muscular. Another has a cowboy moustache and a mane of black. The fifth one nurses the great gash that I put on his face, but he's brandishing a bowie knife. I'm wearing flippers and scuba-gear, and I'm out of breath. Neither fighting nor fleeing is an option.

"What do you want?" I ask.

"We want to get paid," the cowboy tells me. "Now get inside."

With his gun he waves me through a door. My feet slap awkwardly on the ground with each step. I'm inside a cozy, carpeted room with a desk and a laptop computer. A couple couches against the walls and big picture windows. A man in a grey suit stands by the computer pointing a pistol at me. He has fine posture, and silver in his brown hair. "Lose the scuba gear," he says in an annoyed tone. "You're done swimming tonight."

Flippers, suit, and air-tank all go in a pile beside the desk. A pool of water spreads out on the orange-red carpet. He motions for me to sit at the desk, where somebody has placed the third copy of that familiar piece of paper. "My favourite contract," I say. "Where do I sign? Give me a nice, sharp pencil."

"In a moment," the man says. "Based on our clients' embarrassing string of failures, we decided to buy some insurance."

"I like insurance too," I say, locking eyes. I wonder how long it will take for my pilot to deliver my backup.

He smiles. "About that. Boys, bring him in!"

I turn my head to see two of the bald men escorting my own helicopter pilot. He walks with a limp, and his handsome face is heavily bruised.

"Sorry, boss," he mutters. "No backup tonight."

I shake my head. "It's my fault," I tell him. "I walked into this trap."

The cowboy lifts his bowie knife, and sinks it deep into my pilot's throat. Windpipe and arteries open up to create a crimson curtain of thick blood as this victim of my carelessness coughs his last splattered breath and slumps to the floor. My hands tighten on the desk, but I force myself to stay calm. I remind myself that this is a game, I must not lose control, but the glassy eye of my trusted employee reminds me of the stakes.

"Your insurance policy has been cancelled," the grey-suit man says. "Now you can review ours."

"Are you Mr. Jasserty?" I ask him.

He shakes his head, smiling. "No. We're just a small group of professional freelancers hired to do a job our client couldn't do himself. Some tasks require specialization. Now, take a look at the computer screen."

I open up the laptop and see a familiar face. "Hello, Rusty."

There is a moment of lag before the handsome blond spy responds. "Hi. How's the weather in Texas, Julius?"

"How's your asshole?" I ask him.

There is a lag before he grimaces. "Okay then. Look, my boss wants you to sign that contract and then to keep quiet until he liquidates all your assets, you understand? You've got a lot of equipment in that volcano and he wants to take it all or sell it before he starts mining. We can't have you complaining to the government, or trying to get the land back. It would also complicate things if you turn up dead so shortly after signing over the land. We realize now that you're a little bit fucking crazy. So, as your friends there have probably already told you, we got some insurance."

Into the frame walks my whole world. Stephanie Cinnamon, light brown hair and big hazel eyes. Tape across her mouth so she can't speak but I can read her eyes. Eagle's eyes with no fear. Bound and gagged but still somehow hunting. "I'll fix this," I tell her.

Rusty's hand grips, massages her shoulder with too much familiarity. "We'll let her go as soon as we've taken everything out of the volcano," he tells me. "In the meantime I promise to show her the same kindness that you showed me."

My eye twitches, but I keep calm. "Let me speak to her, and I'll sign whatever you want."

He rips the tape off her mouth and she says, "Daddy, don't do a fucking thing they ask. Let them kill us, but don't sign anything! These pieces of shit don't deserve it."

I can't help but laugh. "Did they hurt you?"

"Just my pride."

"I'm going to sign it," I tell her in a defeated

voice, "and we'll build something new together. You'll understand when you have kids of your own."

I take a deep breath. Hold it. Slowly exhale. I used to own a cat. For a toy I tied a string onto a wooden stick with a scrap of cloth at the end of the string. She would chase the scrap of cloth as I bounced it around like a puppet. But if I let the scrap rest, she would just stare at it for awhile before pouncing. The calm before the storm. Those few seconds were always tense. I always knew she was about to attack the stationary scrap of cloth; I was anticipating it and trying to be ready to jerk the prey away from her claws. And yet her attack was always a surprise. Would she wait one second? Ten seconds? Something in between? Her stillness was mesmerizing, and no oracle could predict the moment of her assault. She always caught the scrap. So today I take another page from the book of nature's predatory beasts. I am utterly calm, perhaps even appearing defeated. Mesmerize them with my stillness. We can hear the water lapping against the hull of the boat. Will I wait one second? Ten?

I flip the desk like a log-thrower and kick the cowboy in the balls so hard I can feel his pelvis shatter. Then I grab my discarded oxygen tank and prance backwards, just to keep moving. A hearty swing and I brain the man in the grey suit as he fires blindly with his pistol, hitting a muscular bald man in the shoulder. My daughter is laughing through the little speakers in the toppled laptop. I throw the oxygen tank at one of the four men who still block my exit and grab the gun from the brained man and crouch behind the desk. They're aiming at a moving target, but mine is stationary. A bullet in the oxygen tank provides a deafening roar. The blast-wave topples me onto the couch and I'm pummelled with debris. Pieces of the desk and somebody's arm whack me painfully. I can't hear anything over the ringing in my ears, except for Stephanie's continued mirth. I peer through the cloud of vapour, looking for survivors. There are none. The wall is splattered with blood. Body parts like a jigsaw puzzle.

I rush to the laptop, hoping Stephanie can give me some clue before Rusty cuts the line. Rusty stands in front of her, glaring. "What's going on there?"

Behind him Stephanie says, "Daddy! Felix Rasskakov is-"

The connection is cut before she can finish.

Are there other people on the boat? I need to get out of here. I grab the laptop, the contract, and a pistol. There's nobody out on the deck, and I'm delighted to see that they've tied my stolen boat to this larger one. I retrieve my dynamite and bring it to the rear of the yacht. With the long wick burning I race to my smaller boat and motor away. Somehow this explosion doesn't seem as loud, probably because now I'm back out in the open air and it's not confined to a tiny room. But I'm glad to see the larger boat sinking behind me. Evidence of my presence will hopefully be washed away in the salt water.

They thought they could control me with my daughter. They thought I would tap out and submit. My responsibility is to teach her relentlessness through example. Nobody will give you an inch. Everybody wants blood. The stronger you are the more they rip your flesh.

I have a date with Felix Rasskakov.

Chapter 11

But first I need more clues. How was my daughter kidnapped? Wasn't she on my own property, with a security staff? I'll have their incompetent heads!

On my way to the airport, in a taxi, I call Jesse in lieu of dead Wallace. "Where is my daughter?"

"I'm not sure," he answers casually. "I haven't seen her for a few days. She comes and goes."

"Has she left the mountain?"

"I don't think so. She's probably up in her cabin."

"Find her," I demand, "or you're fired."

"Umm..." he says.

I hang up. Of course he won't find her, and so I will fire him.

It is a hard drive up the hill to my mountain home. The wind howls and I can barely see through the thick wall of blowing white snow. A single snowflake is so gentle, but a trillion of them are a white menace. The sun is up there somewhere, illuminating the distant clouds, but I'm trapped inside a pillow. If I were less disciplined the rage would overcome me as my truck struggles up the incline, getting stuck more than once in the thick layer of snow. But I harness that hate and turn it into a steady drive. I need my energy. I relish the challenge. My daughter is in peril, every piece of my legacy quivers on the precipice, and I have chosen the bold and dangerous course of utter domination. Zero sum motherfuckers. And mother nature slows me down with this hellish storm. Or maybe, I ponder as a screaming gust sways the truck, maybe she is cheering me on.

I stomp into the house and slam shut the door. No smell of roasted eagle today. Jesse rushes to me, blond curls bouncing, and I hate the nervousness in his expression as he hesitates. Finally he says, "I- I couldn't find her. Ah, her truck is still here, so..."

"Did you check the cabin she built?" I glare at him and he squirms.

"She's not there."

"Take me there now."

We bundle up in fur and forge knee-deep paths through the sea of white. Up a steep hill, across a small plain, through a trail in the woods, and over a smaller hill before we finally find a humble little log cabin set snugly into a thicket. This is the first time I've seen her handiwork, and I wonder where she learned to build such a structure. She felled all these trees? Hacked them down, cut them to fit, layered them together? She's strong but she couldn't do this alone.

The roof is made of smaller logs. Moss and mud is packed between them. The stone chimney, rising in the back, is built of mountain rocks cemented together. A snow drift has gathered against one wall, reaching halfway up to the roof. Even the front door is made of small logs lashed together. The only things not hand-built are the pane of glass embedded in the small window, and the metal umbrella covering the chimney's opening.

"She built this herself?" I yell at Jesse over the wind. He merely shrugs. Useless idiot. How did I come to hire him? Inside we find respite from the storm, and great bear skins covering the dirt-floor.

I would expect the whistling of wind finding cracks between the logs, but either Stephanie has patched them perfectly with moss, or the snow-drift has covered them. Jesse lights two oil lamps, though there is also a generator and a lone light bulb hanging from the central rafter. The place is snug and no snow enters, except a little bit which has collected in the fireplace at the far end. Between here and there are two hand-made tables, covered tight with leather to provide a flat surface, and a pile of furs that might serve as a huge bed. I spy baskets, articles of women's clothing, and racks holding guns and bows. Three video cameras watch us from the corners of the room.

I try to count how many furs are here, and from how many species of animal, but I lose track. "How many creatures has she murdered to make this little home?"

"How many trees, too?" Jesse says.

I glare at him. "Help me search the place for clues," I say. "She's been kidnapped."

"Kidnapped? By who?"

"That's what we need to find out."

A laptop rests on one of the tables. And large Tupperware containers full of paperwork beneath that same table. I lift up the container and place it on the table. Inside are several folders packed with paperwork. They each contain maps and documents about geographic locations, their country's legal status, and resources to be extracted. Was she planning to buy property? With what money? Oh dear, what is this? A map of my property in the Congo. With permanent marker she has crossed an X over the volcano which houses Agartha, and a second X on the place where I battled Gavin's men on Felix's property.

Is my own daughter behind these plots? It makes no sense. What is mine is inherently hers. Everything I'm building will be passed down to her. I just wanted for her to live her own life and gain experience before I burdened her with the responsibilities of my scientific utopia. What can I do now? I can't murder my own daughter, but if she's responsible for so many deaths, I may never be able to forgive her.

What bothers me most is that she left this evidence so open to discovery in a mere plastic container. How could she ever hope to pull off such a heist if she won't even try to cover her tracks? But indeed, she pulled it off. And now what's this business about her being kidnapped? Is that a lie? I look at the cameras and wonder if she's watching me from some secret location. I hold the maps up for the cameras to see. "Stephanie! Where are you? What's the meaning of this?"

There's more going on here. Why did Alex's men lead me to Felix's mine in Africa? Why did I keep coming across the name Blackburn? Maybe somebody planted this evidence when they kidnapped Stephanie. Or maybe she wanted me to find it, as a way of gaining my attention. I have always been a vagabond, but I always made time for her when she was a child.

A buzz in my pocket tells me I have a text message. It is from Armand. "The long siege is over. Agartha is yours, Mr. Cinnamon. We quarantine many virus. Save or delete?"

Finally some good news! I wish I had the means to fully repay those who were loyal. But instead, I have to ask even more of my dear Armand. "Save one for study. Delete the rest. I need your help again, if you are up to it."

"Always," comes his quick reply.

I juggle puzzle pieces in my brain and lay out a plan. My thumbs articulate Armand's part in that plan. "Jesse!" I snap. He turns his head from where he was stupidly studying a pile of clothes hanging on a chair. "You can keep your job, but I want you to check this out for me. I've brought a laptop which received a live video feed from whoever kidnapped Stephanie. Find out what you can about where the video came from. Okay?"

He only nods. In truth he's not stupid, but I'm still pissed that she was stolen during his watch. Now I need to hit the gym, get some sleep, and prepare transportation to coincide with Armand.

Chapter 12

It feels I have time-travelled back more than a century. Felix Rasskakov's impressive country estate is just north of an abandoned Russian town and south of a small mountain range. Other local land-owning families have long since abandoned their own mansions, which have fallen to ruin. But Felix renovated his and expanded on the original property. Now he has forests for hunting, lakes for swimming and boating, a helicopter pad and small-plane runway so he can reach civilization, and a radio tower.

His actual house, larger than my own dwelling, appears tiny as the brick structure is dwarfed by the sprawling lawn, yet the brown bricks stand out stark against the snow. Three stories high with rows of rectangular windows reflecting the frost, white trim, and a regale balcony to greet the lonely lawn. A black iron fence protects the mansion on the front and both sides, but the fence disappears into the forest in back. All this I can see through binoculars from the church tower in the abandoned town across the frozen, winding river.

I have a small crew for this affair. Four men to swarm the front gates and trigger the alarms while I sneak in through the back. A full day of recon has shown us that Felix's biggest security advantage is how open this estate is, and so that forest in the rear represents a vulnerability. Something tells me my daughter is inside that mansion, or somewhere in the forest beyond. If anything has happened to her I will lament that later. Right now her well-being depends on me staying focused.

Armand is on his way with a special package. If I fail he will finish what I started.

Well before nightfall I take to the cover of the trees which conceal my northerly trek up the western flank of the vast plain. I cross the frozen river on foot and arc around to approach the property from the north. The northern fence is just as tall here in the woods, but nobody can see me as I snip away enough sections to slip through with my weapons and gear. But I do not slip through yet. Instead I find a place to sleep with my sleeping bag, beneath a great fallen tree. I sleep easy and wake when my phone vibrates in my hand. It's time.

Run through the fresh gap in the fence. Clean air fills my lungs and the snow-crusted evergreens dwarf me like friendly giants. Starlight sparkles off the fluffy multitude of crystal freeze. I go as quietly as crunchy winter allows. I pass a snowmobile parked alongside a log cabin in the woods, similar in structure to Stephanie's. Has he put her to work so quickly? A paranoid voice in my head suggests collusion between the two scoundrels. I will give my daughter a chance to explain. I will give Felix his own brain in a blender.

Now I'm at the edge of the treeline, peering into Felix's back yard. There is a gazebo, a heated pool, and several leafless trees waiting patiently for summer. I look for any windows that may be illuminated. A single rectangle of light blasts yellow from the top floor, and a figure is vaguely visible, sitting at a desk.

My men all confirm they are in position. I give the signal via wireless, then I sprint from my hiding spot and swoop across the darkest patches of the lawn. Barely have my feet touched the ground when I hear explosions and gunfire erupt on the front lawn. Flashes light up the sky, and more dark rectangles turn to yellow as the house awakes from its slumber.

With a silenced pistol I shoot out a downstairs window and climb through into the darkness. I hear voices, and someone barking orders in Russian elsewhere in the expansive home. I realize it would be funny if Felix wasn't even home and I murdered all his staff. And burned down his house.

I'm in a dining room. The long wooden table may be as old as the house. A dormant light hangs from the ceiling under a shade of a hundred beautiful stained-glass panes. The doors are framed with carved wood. Even in shadow this house is a work of art but I can't take the time to appreciate it. Feet are clomping down the stairs.

I remain hidden. Now beneath the table, now behind a bookshelf, treading softly on rugs, listening for the familiar sound of Felix's voice. I can hear him upstairs. I don't know Russian so I don't know what he's saying, but he is unnervingly calm considering the continued blasts and gunshots emanating from outside.

My every nerve tingles as I step up the stairs. My padded footwear is made for stealth. A shadow appears. The silhouette of Felix Rasskakov looks down at me. I can see his broad shoulders and even his beard as he turns his head. God, he could be me! Though he's ten years younger and has ten pounds more muscle.

"We have things to discuss, old friend," he says, in the lowest tone possible. It's like a boat's engine idling in the water.

I let my knives speak instead. They glint ever so briefly as they twirl almost silently through the air. He bats them aside and steps down onto the first step. I see he's wearing a suit, even at this early hour. "I do not like what you have done to my mine," he says, "and I do not like what you are doing to my home."

"I don't like what you've done to my daughter."

"I was never this rough with her."

When I throw two more knives it's just to buy enough time to pull out a small pistol. But he's fast as lightning and already lunging at me before I can aim. I duck, hugging the stairs so he sails over me. Turn around. I tread backwards up the stairs, aiming down. But Felix has disappeared. Now he's hunting me in his own home. My cover is blown. I wanted to take him down fast.

"Where's Stephanie?" I demand.

"I don't know!" he calls back from somewhere downstairs, voice echoing through the halls. "Stop this nonsense so we can speak!"

Speak indeed, while your employees surround and dismember me. Will they demand again that I sign their contract? I have a better plan. I find an office with a waste basket full of paper. A couple matches help to brighten the room! This building is brick on the outside, but the inside is all wood, and much of it is old. The master bedroom provides me with cologne and a closet full of fine clothes. Soon I have no reason to be jealous of his flaming wardrobe.

On my way to the next room I receive a kick in the face. My nose is a ruin and blood pours into my mouth. I do a backwards tumble but Felix is on top of me, and I am disoriented and caught off guard. We roll around on the ground, each one seeking definitive dominance over the other, and I can hear the roar of flames from the rooms I've visited. He towers over me, straddling me and seeking to land punches. His fist finds the side of my head. I jab his thigh repeatedly. Flames illuminate his beastly, snarling face. Even his scars are better than mine, cutting through his beard like the road leading through the jungle to Agartha. With the memory of Agartha I find new strength and roll him onto his side. We knock over a decorative table in the hall. A vase smashes on the dark-stained hardwood, and Felix rolls me onto the shards which dig into shoulders still healing from the falcon's talons. But I relish the pain and scrape my fingers across his face. Our legs are intertwined. He bites my pinky finger and I can't get it out. Finally I roar as I feel the bone break, and he rips the entire finger from my hand.

Fuelled by adrenaline I smash my elbow into his face over and over and over. The fallen table has caught fire and we can both feel the heat. He grabs a piece of the shattered vase and jabs it at my eye. I dodge so he barely misses, but as I grab his wrist his other hand finds my throat. His fingers are thick and long, seeking to crush rather than strangle. But I have a piece of vase too, and it sinks deep into his wrist. Down the road kids, not across! Blood pours from the serious wound. Somehow he shoves me off him, and leaps through the flames. Now I can't see which room he's got to, but this whole floor is lost to the fire. I grab a piece of the vase which is blackened in flame, and I use it to cauterize the stump of my missing finger.

I head downstairs. If I can reach the back yard before him then I'll have him pinned. But when I jump outside I see him already disappearing into the woods. I hear helicopters. I race after my prey.

The winter forest is so peaceful. I can barely hear the crackle of the burning house behind me. Luckily that same flame illuminates my path and shows me Felix's footprints. I follow them warily, wondering how they're not accompanied by a stream of wrist-blood. He is a clever fox. They lead me, almost predictably, back to the log cabin I'd spotted earlier. But the trail of footprints don't lead me to the entrance. Instead they stop at a the stone outcropping of an old-style well. I resist the urge to look over the edge, since he must be hiding within. Instead I pace around the thing, looking for evidence for where he has gone. It is a picturesque well, plastered with ice which is coated with snow. It's very wide but I can't see how deep. A wooden roof protects the tunnel from birdshit and falling leaves. A light wind rustles the bare branches in the darkness above, nature's lonesome communication saying hello while not pretending to be my friend.

Something shoves me and I tumble forward into the well. My hands reach out and I barely grab the other side. I dangle. My missing finger throbs. Down below I can just see the light shimmer of distant ice, deep enough to break my legs. Something glints in the moonlight. It is the blade of an axe, swinging for my hands. I grab the wooden pole and hang from that by one hand, and the axe sparks off the stone with a sharp clink and a scrape. How to escape? I reach up with my injured hand and painfully wrap four fingers around a beam below the little roof. The swinging axe cracks the pole I had just been holding, and my weight pulls the roof down, straining the opposite pole. The cauterization fails and blood pours from my stump. The axe shatters the other pole and the roof and me drop two feet. Now the whole wooden construction is jammed awkwardly in the mouth of the well and I hang from it, unable to see the outside except through a little slit between stone and wood. Felix's face appears in this little slit. If I wasn't holding on with both hands I would throw another knife at him.

"Maybe now we can talk," he says.

"This was a good fight," I tell him. If he kills me now he has earned his victory, and I only lament the fate of my daughter and the sweet dream of Agartha.

"I should have known you would overreact," he rasps.

"Overreact? You robbed me and killed my men!"

"I killed nobody!"

"You kidnapped my daughter!"

"Kidnapped- *what?*" He peers closer through the crack and I see genuine confusion on his face, illuminated by the distant flames which have increased in their Hellish intensity.

A new sound enters the scene. It is the fludding of helicopter blades. My cavalry has arrived, but are they too late to save me?

"*Verdammt!*" Felix chokes, looking into the sky. Machine guns pierce the growing cacophony, and Felix flees the rain of bullets which pelt the snow.

The next thing I hear is Armand calling out, "Mr Cinnamon!"

"In here!" I boom. "In the well!"

Now I can safely reach up and grab the stony edge. Armand and two more men lift the battered roof and help me out of the well. "Where did he go?" I snap, looking around for Felix. His trail leads toward the cabin.

"Your finger, Mr. Cinnamon!" Armand scolds me, like I've carelessly traipsed mud upon his carpet. I ignore him and start after Felix again, but

Armand shouts, "He has a snowmobile! You cannot chase him!"

Indeed I can now see the tracks of the snowmobile. Two helicopters hover above us. "Tell one of them to scout the forest. Try to find Felix Rasskakov! Bring him to me alive."

Armand snaps orders into the lapel of his fluffy winter jacket and one of the choppers tilts its nose, heading out on patrol and shining a big spotlight.

I clasp his shoulder. "Did you retrieve the package?"

He nods. "It is in the helicopter." He grins. "It is not very happy."

We all fly away from the burning house. I learn that Felix's staff have already surrendered. No casualties tonight, except my finger, which means I have several live conduits of information to squeeze. I'll have to learn something useful from this adventure. Also present in the chopper is my other long-time business colleague, Viktor Sabitov, one-eyed, tied up, and nearly drooling with anger at having been kidnapped from his home. I ignore his complaints, preferring not to talk in the noisy vehicle. I merely pat his old face and say, "We'll talk in some quieter place."

That quieter place is the dusty old church in the abandoned town. Most of the pews have been burnt by squatters for firewood in the blackened fireplace, and between the few remaining ones are the meagre belongings of the vagrants who we've temporarily displaced. Sleeping bags, dented metal kitchenware, syringes. The stained-glass of the tall windows have been replaced with wood. The silhouette of a long-gone pipe-organ is still visible against the back wall of the stage. I have untied the disgruntled old man and return to him his cane so he can walk over the rubble, and sit in one of the pews for a nice long conversation.

I sit in a feeble foldable metal chair and face him. "When you called me Mr. Blackburn, why did you do that?" I ask.

But he's in no mood to answer my questions. He leans forward and bangs his cane on the floor, which echoes throughout the cavernous ruin. There is no fear in this man, acting like he isn't surrounded by five dark-skinned killers from the mighty jungle, and one crazy billionaire who's been grinding up humans like meat. Armand's men look regale in long, navy-blue wool jackets, their breath puffing white in the air. Viktor stares me down with his one good eye and his disconcerting black electronic glass eye. "Why did you take me from my home? Who do you think you are, *Mr Blackburn?*"

"There is is again," I say. "You know my name is Julius Cinnamon. Stop playing games, old friend."

"Old friends visit and talk, not steal us from our homes!" His cane stabs the floor three more times. "Why did you burn down Felix's house? Why did you kidnap me and bring me here?" He indicates the ugly environment we've chosen for this parlay.

I hold out my injured hand and start counting on my fingers. "One, I caught a man spying on me. Two, I caught a woman spying on my property in Africa. Three, my guards staged a mutiny and robbed my property, killing my employees. Four, somebody kidnapped my daughter. Five... this missing finger."

His expression changes, losing some of the spite and anger. He looks like he just remembered that he's speaking to a fellow human. "I did not know all this." He gulps. "I am sorry."

"So you had nothing to do with any of that?"

"I sent a woman to take pictures on your African property. You would not tell us what you were doing, and we had to find out." He punctuates this with a cane-stab on the floor. "But she took my money and never did the job. That is all I did."

"I caught her," I say. "She died for your sins."

The anger returns. "What about your sins? Surely they are much worse than mine!"

"Maybe. We can get discuss my sins later. But where did you hear the name Blackburn?"

"A long time ago, before you were born."

Now I'm intrigued. "Go on."

"I am the oldest in my family. My youngest sibling was a sweet, pretty girl. *Jasmina*. But she wasn't right in the head." He stabs his own head viciously with a crooked finger. "She spoke to God, had a mission from God, listened to angels, dreamed nightmares of devils. So she became a nun, you see? Can you guess where we sent her? Which convent Jasmina lived in? I think you know about your father, the deals he made. The convents which were his playthings. My sweet little sister."

This is too much. I understood the whole story as soon as he mentioned her name. "Jasmina is my mother," I whisper to my uncle.

"Was," he reminds me. "And how did you know her name?"

"My uncle told me. My other uncle. My father's brother. How long have you known who I am?"

"Very recently. Your brother found me."

"I have no brothers."

"You do," Viktor says. "You probably have many, but your father only raised one child other than yourself. A younger man, Samuel Blackburn, who was very interested in your affairs. He sought me out and told me who you are."

"Why did he find you to tell you that? What did he want from you?"

Viktor shakes his head slowly. "Sly boy, or so he thinks. He throws a wrench in your gears. He thinks he can make me into your enemy. I hate your father for what he did to my sister, and so I hate half of you. Your very existence represents that violation! When I met him, I could see it in his eyes, that he was testing to see if I hated you enough to help him destroy you. What you have built, he wants it for himself, even though he has never met you."

I peer at him with a sense of doubt. "This is a lie. You expect me to accept that you've been my secret uncle for all these years? It's an unbelievable coincidence."

He laughs. "It is no coincidence. Did I seek you out to help you buy land? Were we introduced by a mutual friend? No. You found me because I lived close to where your mother lived. Felix's family comes from this town, so similar to mine." As he speaks his thumb rubs the shiny knob of his cane's handle.

"I sought you out because of the strength of your businesses," I correct him. "I wanted to succeed!"

"You came back as Julius Cinnamon, to erase wounds, to make something good where your father created ugliness. You know what you are. You were drawn to the homeland of your dead mother."

Ancient, insatiable frustration overwhelms me. I stand and hurl my chair across the sacred space of the church. It twirls in an arc and bangs against the distant stone wall, clanging down onto the floor. "A child of rape!" I scream, grasping the pew with white knuckles. "An infection! Filthy worm with hate in my blood."

I am leaning against a pew, staring down at the dirty floor. No thoughts may enter my mental space, just hate and disgust twisting my heart. How can I ever escape my creation? No matter what I do, I was forged in ugliness. And how much I enjoy to dominate others, to watch my enemies die. The beast. Murderer. Julius Cinnamon is a lie. I am Julius Blackburn, horror monster and murderer, twisted and scarred.

Viktor is on his feet, his cane clacking on the floor as he hobbles over to me. "You acted with a noble cause," he tells me. "You abandoned your father and his legacy, and started your own. You are violent and cruel like him, but I also see my young sister in your eyes. I am your uncle. Let me be your friend."

Armand speaks. "You are a king, Mr. Cinnamon. I have never known a greater man. Agartha is your gift to the world. You are a beast and we will crush your enemies."

"He did this," I mutter. "Samuel Blackburn, my false brother who is too cowardly to face me. He's trying to ruin my plans."

"Let's stop him," Viktor says, rubbing the cap

of his cane. "You are part of my family, and so is your daughter."

Enough wallowing. I have work to do. Family to rescue. Family to kill. I take my phone from my pocket and call Jesse, to see if he has discovered any clues from the laptop.

As I dial the number, I see Viktor pop open his cane's cap, revealing a nest of little pills like eggs. He reaches in and pulls out a small white capsule, places it on his tongue. Swallows.

"My heart," he explains.

Chapter 13

We are on another planet, an ice-world where a day lasts half a year. People only come here to do scientific research, and to die. I come for love and vengeance.

Our five snowmobiles leave tracks across the Antarctic plain of a permanently frozen lake. Snow dunes dissolve wispy into the turbulent air, the skirt of the world, and cover our tracks almost as soon as they are made. The frigid outline of mountains in the distance beckons me. My saw-tooth saviour, protecting my stolen daughter from my aggressors. The Ice-Queen awaiting her father's revenge. The wind doesn't howl, it rumbles and scrapes my face. Our machines are not fuelled with gas or electricity, but by a symphony. This landscape is an orchestra and we live in its clamorous music. The great composers had mountains and expanses like this in their hearts. My heart will not feel joy until I see Stephanie unharmed, and bury my treacherous secret brother in ice. I'll shatter his frozen blood as a sacrifice to the composer and conductor of this adventure.

Jesse couldn't find an IP address where Rusty's ransom video originated. Instead he found satellite coordinates which led us here to the south end of the Earth. Beasts, we leave behind civilization and safety. This is Jesse's chance to redeem himself for allowing Stephanie to go missing on his watch. Armand is with us too, and two of his best men. Felix has escaped us for now. His own snowmobile tracks are hidden in fresh snowfall near the other end of the world.

She is somewhere in those mountains. What kind of building is she in? Is my brother there, too? Or is he out concocting other schemes? Do they have a little research trailer, a tin can like the science-stations near the coast? Or has my hostile brother built a stronger compound of metal and cement? Perhaps the Blackburns now have a new castle in this cold continent which is almost as frosty as our father's heart. My biggest fear is that there is no compound here at all. Maybe the signal was somehow re-routed here from some other location, and my daughter is with her captors far away. My second biggest fear is that I won't be able to find my way in. What if it's underground? Where is the entrance? We've brought enough explosives and firepower to knock down any wall. But we can't bring down a mountain.

We fly in a v-shape towards our destination. I am in the lead flanked by Armand and Jesse. Armand's friends take up the rear. It is colder than cold, ice forming on my beard. But we have the best clothes and the wind is at our backs.

I feel a deep rumble in the ice beneath my vehicle. Sudden explosions surround us and send quakes across the frozen lake. A cracking noise echoes from everywhere like a continent snapped in half. Plumes of ice-shards blast into the sky. A smoky mist obscures the outside world. More than a dozen detonations form a circle around us.

"A booby trap!" Armand screams.

The world is tilting and breaking apart. The blasts have ripped and cracked through the many feet of thick ice, and now we are racing across an ice-island. No, two islands! Three! We're all split up, twisted around, and set in different directions. My chunk of ice is sinking in the rear and rising up ahead of me. I stand on two feet and gun the engine. It roars! I see one of Armand's men behind me fall screaming into the deadly-cold water. His snowmobile makes one splash and he makes a smaller one amidst the churning chunks of ice like a cup of cola.

My chunk of ice continues to tilt until I'm almost vertical, but then I shoot off the tip and into the still-dissipating mist and smoke of the explosions. I am arcing through the air, preparing for a harsh landing on the flat surface beyond. But as I come through the other side I see that it's not flat at all. The fracture lines have extended outward, creating several smaller islands surrounding the circle of blasts. Just as I have escaped an island tilting upwards, I am headed for another tilting down! My back-end touches down with deceptive gentleness, and my front slams down like a hammer. It almost breaks my wrists, almost sends me hurtling from my vehicle. But I keep my grip. But now I'm headed for the hungry waters, frothing and splashing with their unexpected turbulence, and a sheer wall of ice stands beyond it, taller than a man. There's nothing to do but stand on the seat and, at the last minute, leap from my snowmobile as it hits the water. The force of my jump is not as strong as the momentum transferred to me from the abandoned machine. I'm launched upwards at the wall of ice before me, and I barely grab the ledge. I hold on with one hand, even as it crumbles in my grip. I scramble with the other hand, both hands, and somehow keep a hold! To my left I see Armand flying through the air, laughing just before he makes a hard landing beyond my vision.

I pull myself up, relieved to see that now I am indeed safely beyond the region of cracked up and exploded ice. Behind me, shining chunks like icebergs are still scraping and rolling against each other, churning up the hidden lake below. Armand's other man struggles to keep hold of the tip of one piece, right in the inaccessible centre of the pit. It keeps rolling and rolling until he's horribly crushed between two pieces which crumble and shatter like glass. I shake my head and add two more names to the list of those who deserve vengeance from Samuel Blackburn and Felix Rasskakov.

Jesse has survived, but like me he has lost his snowmobile. Only Armand's machine has made it out of the fray, and it lays on its side now with Armand a dozen feet away laying on his back and staring up into the blue sky.

"Are you hurt?" I ask, kneeling beside him.

Armand shakes his head. "I am counting my blessings," is all he says.

"I p-pissed myself," Jesse stammers. He kneels on the other side of Armand.

"Jesus Christ," I say. "You'll freeze your cock

off!"

"Thought I was gonna die."

"We'll get you a fucking diaper next time."

I push the remaining snowmobile back up onto its feet, but one of the front skis is broken.

Armand asks, "What was the trigger for that trap?"

I shake my head. "I didn't notice anything." Which means we won't be able to avoid another one, since we don't know what to look for.

"We're almost to the mountains," Jesse says.

"We will go slow and keep an eye out for anything, pressure plates or trip wires," Armand instructs.

He kneels and says a prayer for his fallen comrades. Then the three of us climb onto the snowmobile with Armand driving. Jesse and I hang on like children. The wounded vehicle veers hard to the right so Armand has to correct it by steering to the left. It's a slow, strenuous ride. I have the location mapped on my phone. "Into that valley," I say, and Armand uses the awkward steering to bring us into a frozen fjord. Dark blue-grey cliffs tower above us on both sides. I wonder if we'll be able to find our way inside before Jesse's piss-soaked pants turn him into a eunuch or a corpse.

At the end of this little valley the gaping entrance is obvious. The mountain drives straight up from the flat surface of the snow-covered lake, and a massive hole is cut out of the rock, as tall and wide as a hangar. It is a dark treasure leading inside the mountain. At first I wonder how it does not fill up with snow, but then I see that the blowing swirls of white avoid the area, pushed away by some wind emanating from within. When we finally approach we can feel the warmer breeze pushing softly and steadily.

It's necessary to abandon the snowmobile. The crooked driving will not serve inside the down-sloping tunnel. It's wide enough for a four-lane highway. The walls and curved ceiling are reinforced with steel and cement, illuminated by embedded lights. Way down, it turns to the right.

We stand in a row and look deep into our enemy's orifice. Does Samuel Blackburn own this? My father is a rich man, but I doubt he would give Samuel enough for such a construction project. The cracks in the cement suggest this may be from a previous decade. Has he purchased it? Is he squatting in an abandoned compound? I remind myself that I don't truly know who has kidnapped my daughter, who owns Jasserty Holdings, or what to expect inside.

Just before we enter Armand points above us to something hanging from the frosty frame of the entrance. Dangling from a string a dozen feet above us is a chunk of flesh. It is the cock and balls from some poor castrated man, and they are strung up like a trophy or a warning. I almost want to give them a proper burial. "What kind of hideous freaks are we dealing with?" They sway and turn slightly, tossed around gently in that place where the moaning outside wind battles the softer breeze from within the tunnel.

Soon our footsteps echo off the walls and the wind from outside takes on a haunted aspect as its wailing ghost calls to us, warning us not to enter into the lions' den. We don't heed its call but proceed warily, rifles out and eyes peeled. We pass by a steel door with no handle, no way to open it. One of the lights above flickers. It's still cold. There are occasional patches of ice. But the wind that blows gently from below is so much warmer than the hostile germ-killing atmosphere we just left.

Warmer and warmer, and the tunnel starts to curve. More doors with no handles. I'm extremely curious about what's beyond those doors. Are we headed into another Agartha with a network of extended tunnels and rooms beyond the main cut? How fitting, that my subterranean Valhalla lives in the lush jungle while my secret brother has his buried in ice.

What is generating this heat? We pause to loosen our collars, and I can finally smell the dank stench of Jesse's pissed pants. I wonder if there is a thermal duct at the terminus of this ride, fed by deep primordial core-heat. In how many places are we tapping this vein?

"Look there." Jesse points ahead of us. "Somebody's waiting."

A man in a black uniform stands in the middle of the road, just now visible around the ever-curving road-path. Decision time. Do we speak with him or kill him? We didn't come here to negotiate, so I drop to one knee and take aim with my rifle.

"I wouldn't do that," a voice warns from behind. I turn and see two men emerging from around the bend. They wear the same black uniforms, with a red emblem on the chest, and they're armed. At the same time a door opens on my left and a man and a woman come out to join their buddies.

"Surrounded," I curse.

"Drop those guns, faggots!" The woman commands. Her short blond hair is cut in a square that's almost as sharp as the lines of her masculine jaw.

I resist the urge to ignore her, the urge to open fire. There is no calculation here that allows me to defeat them.

I lay down the rifle. "You have us," I admit.

"Split apart," the blond woman says.

I shake my head. "Nope." I know that I'm the only one of any value to them, and they may just murder my last two companions. So we three cluster together, back-to-back, arms in the air.

"You don't want to fuck with me," the Bitch

snaps.

"Then why did I come here?"

A gunshot cracks the air and the cement at my feet explodes in a little puff of cement-splinters. "I'll put a bullet in your dick you smart-mouthed brat. *Split the fuck apart and lay down!*"

Suddenly I'm imagining her naked, her muscles covered in oil. I'd wrestle her to the ground and spread her legs, show her who's boss. I think she can read my thoughts because now she snarls, losing her temper, and stomps over to us in her big sexy boots. "The more you try to act like a man," I say, "the more your womanly vulnerability shines through!"

She raises the butt of her rifle to crack me on the head, but Jesse leaps on her before I get the chance! He shoves the up-raised weapon backwards and pulls out a hidden knife.

Sadly, she is much faster. Somehow she has already buried a knife in his ribs. He collapses into my arms and she backs away, rifle aimed.

"Goddammit," I grumble, holding my wounded soldier. Her knife is still stuck in Jesse's side, and I leave it there so it won't gush more blood.

"If I wanted you dead," she said, "You'd all be fucking dead. Now lie down on the fucking floor or I'll fuck you with that knife. We have a doctor and we can fix your friend, but only after you submit to my, *womanly will.*"

If I could sacrifice Jesse for victory, I would. If I don't crush these fuckers there will be a never-ending supply of death. But they have us by the balls, and so we lay down on our faces as the guards come and put us in handcuffs. I wait for the bullets that kill Armand and Jesse, but the Bitch is true to her word. Somebody soon arrives with a simple stretcher and carries Jesse away. "God, he pissed himself," one of his carriers complains.

The Bitch kneels down in front of me. I look up at her snarling face. She says, "Cooperation. See how that works? Not everything has to be a bloodbath."

They split us up. Jesse disappears behind one door and Armand and I are taken through another. The bowels within the bowels. It is a smaller service walkway, dimly lit and warmer. We enter an elevator. It descends noisily, not a smooth ride. Armand is taller than any of our captors. He gives me a look to see if I have any tricks up my sleeve, anything to communicate. He expects surprises, plans, and success from his boss. But I have nothing. We are prey. The victors glare at us with steel hatred, surrounding us. I wonder if I have killed somebody they like.

The realization hits me that I may soon meet my young half-brother, Samuel Blackburn. Another offspring of that hateful rapist, my horrible masculine forebear. Will I see myself reflected in him? Which instincts has he nurtured? Which ones has he let atrophy? Is he handsomer than me? His beard as thick? A new idea forms. Can we become allies? If he has any sense he must recognize my power and potential. I can forgive his sins for a brighter future. Unless he's harmed my daughter in any way. I remember the explosives strapped to my chest.

When we arrive at our destination the elevator dings, and I can tell that it's a real bell instead of a digital noise played through cheap speakers. How old is this place?

"Time to meet the Ice Queen," the Bitch whispers in my ear. I can feel her hot breath. I think she likes me.

But wait.

"Ice Queen?" I ask.

We're shoved through the door and into a great control room. The domed ceiling is panels of murky glass in dull pastel colours, arranged in geometric shapes and looking like futuristic stained-glass. Each panel glows, illuminating the scene below. The concave floor is three concentric layers leading to a pit of machinery at the bottom. Each layer of the floor is ringed with rails and computer terminals where the screens are built into the machines. Many of the screens are dark but a few are lit up with the large green and white pixels of a previous generation of computers. Bear skins and deer skins hang from the rails and the dead terminals. Where did they get animal skins in desolate Antarctica? The room is populated by a few worker bees studying their old screens, and more than a dozen loungers leaning against rails with weapons or drinks. At the very bottom I see three naked people, two men and one woman, chained to their machines. They sit with their heads hunched over. They look up with interest when I enter the room, then lower their heads again as their interest disappears. I don't recognize them.

But I do recognize my daughter, Stephanie Cinnamon. She sits in a large chair, like a throne covered in more animal skins, and she stares at me from across the room with the condescending look of an angry queen at a troublesome peasant. Despite the warmth in the room she wears even more animal skins as a robe, and her hair is a big mess. She usually keeps it so neat! She's flanked by two men. One one side is a bald, naked man curled up in a frightened ball. On the other side is Felix Rasskakov, naked and proud with his hairy barrel-chest and beautiful beard. His wrist is heavily bandaged. He looks at me like we're fighters in a pit.

"Move, faggot!" The Bitch says from behind

me, shoving me with the butt of her gun. I walk around the top ring, taking my time and observing everything around me. When Armand and I reach the so-called Ice Queen, she steps down from her throne of furs. When she stands her robe parts slightly and I peripherally perceive that she's naked underneath, hairy of bush and perky of tit, my cave-woman daughter. Felix remains beside her, and so does the shrivelled little man crouching on the floor. She holds the other end of his chain.

"What exactly is going on?" I ask. She's clearly not a captive like I'd been led to believe. "Is Felix Rasskakov just an alias for Samuel Blackburn? Stephanie, I would give everything for you, but if you're behind all this treachery..."

"You ruined my fun, Daddy," she sulks, with overly-serious eyes. "When the bomb went off outside I thought you'd be Uncle Sammy."

I'm not amused. "What the fuck is going on?"

"Wait," the Bitch behind me says. "He's your father?" She quickly removes my handcuffs.

Stephanie sighs and looks down at the slave on the end of her chain. I notice that he's not actually bald, but most of his blond hair has been chopped roughly off. "Stand up, slave," she tells him.

Timidly, the naked man stands. The first thing I notice is that he's freshly a eunuch. Where his dick and balls should be is a blood-soaked bandage with no bulge beneath. I remember the frozen package hanging outside in the entrance. The second thing I notice is that I recognize this man. It's Rusty Knight. His pale face completely lacks the confidence that I stole from him, or the menace that he conveyed when I saw him on the video screen. He won't look me in the eye, and he's developed a nervous twitch. I wonder, what's the difference between pity and disgust?

"You remember what my Daddy did to you, Rusty?" She jerks his chain and he nods. Her voice is so viciously sweet. "Remember when you tried to do the same thing to me, Rusty? You won't be able to do that anymore. You could have left me locked up, like Uncle Sammy told you. But you wanted to fuck me. You wanted to take back what my Daddy took from you. So you came close to me. And then I won."

I've created a monster. "Tell me everything," I say.

Now her shoulders slump. "It's all my fault," she admits, sitting back in the chair.

"It's our fault," Felix corrects her, holding her hand. She squeezes back and they share a meaningful look that I've rarely shared with any lover.

She sighs again, and I know she's sulking to avoid being in trouble with her father.

I roar at her. "You're a fucking grown

woman, just fucking tell me *what the fuck is going on!*"

Felix speaks. "We stole your..."

"Shut the fuck up!" I scream so loud it threatens to tear my throat. "I'm speaking to my daughter!"

"We stole your battery," she says with pride. Now she's leaning forward defiantly, oblivious to her tits hanging out. She's unable to be truly apologetic. She went from sulky to proud, neither of which are the correct attitudes for what she's done. I've failed to teach her the full range of emotions, and she would never learn them up on my mountain.

She continues. "I wanted to be part of your business, but you don't trust me because I'm a girl."

"Bullshit," I retort. "I've given some of my best jobs to women. I already told you, I trust you too much because you're my daughter. I can't see you clearly and my emotions get in the way. I would never know when to fire you. *So you stole the battery and killed my employees?*"

She shakes her head. "We didn't kill anybody. We just wanted to take your battery to prove..."

"What? To fucking prove what?"

Felix says, "To prove that we're bold and strong like Julius Cinnamon. You kept her out of your business and you kept me out of your biggest project. You won't negotiate. Everything you do is a ridiculous spectacle! We wanted to be on your level, so we broke the rules. Just like you would do."

I refuse to respond to him. I don't even know why he's here. So I look back at Stephanie. "Is that true?"

She nods sweetly and I want to forgive her, which makes me even more angry. "We made a deal with Alex," she says. "He gave us information and arranged everything. We just had to pay him and he'd deliver the battery to Felix. Nobody would get hurt. But we didn't know that someone else paid him even more to take more than the battery."

"Samuel Blackburn," I say.

"Uncle Sammy," she agrees. "He wants everything you own."

"You met him?"

"Only after they kidnapped me," she says. "Until then I had no idea what was going on, why Alex never delivered the battery and why I couldn't get in touch with him. They got me while I was out hunting. I guess I was also being hunted. They brought me here and I met your brother. Daddy, he's got money and power, he hires lots of people, and for some reason he just wants to take everything from you. He was really nice to me. He has big plans, and I think he wants me on his side. But he made a mistake and left Rusty in charge."

"What about these people?" I nod towards

the Bitch who stabbed Jesse. "Whose people are they?"

The Bitch answers that question. "Sammy Blackburn paid us money. The Ice Queen offers more than that."

"What did you offer her?" I ask my daughter.

"A place in your glorious empire, after we crush Uncle Sammy."

I can only laugh. Armand laughs, too. "She is surely your daughter, Mister Cinnamon. Your mistake was hiring Alex for money, when the rest of us want a piece of your empire. We are loyal to you, not your dollars!"

"We were going to give the battery back," Felix tells me. His demeanour is serious and matter-of-fact, neither apologetic or confrontational. I burned down his house and he bit off my finger, so we're not exactly best friends. Also, it seems he's been fucking my daughter behind my back.

"How long have the two of you been together?"

Stephanie says, "Do you remember when you had him and Viktor over to the house for dinner, after you sold your Cinnamon patent? We made love that night."

"She was only eighteen!" I hiss at the man who has stolen my daughters' heart.

He can't hide his grin. "I know."

"So after I took Rusty's balls," Stephanie

continues, "I called my man to bring some proper clothes and help me plan how we were going to steal everything back from Uncle Sammy."

"It was going to be a gift," Felix says. "Everything he owns and his head on a platter.

So I was beset on three sides. Viktor sent spies, Felix and my own daughter conspired to rob me of my battery, and my wretched half-brother has taken it all. No wonder I couldn't make any sense of it.

She stands up, but she's staring at the floor. "Daddy, I'm sorry. I'm sort of not sorry, because I don't know how else I could take part in your life, so we could be a team. But also I am sorry, because I didn't act like a team. I'm sorry because Alex got people killed, and I could have told you he was a traitor."

I can tell that it hurts her to apologize. I wonder if she's ever done that before. She still won't look me in the eye, and I keep silent to just let her cook in her own shameful juices. Let her keep feeling bad for a moment, relish the consequences. Taste the world through the shit that comes crashing down when you fuck up hard.

"I'm impressed that you took this place from my brother," I tell her finally. "You caused a lot of trouble for Samuel. But you caused trouble for me, too. So now you can help me put it all back together."

"Also I'm pregnant with Felix," she says. I suck in air through clamped teeth. "And I need you two to be friends."

Felix says, "I have always looked up to-"

"Stop," I inject, extending my good right hand. "I won't replace your house because you can't replace my finger. But she's made a damn good choice."

We shake. My family has grown. My team is huge. "Now, since you've taken Samuel's antarctic base you must have some useful information about what he has planned. What can you tell me about our nemesis?"

She smiles. "Lots and lots."

Chapter 14

Is this the high-rise condominium of a respected biologist? Or the cluttered apartment of a college stoner? My eyes and nose suggest the latter, yet I know the former to be true. I sit on a stool in a corner among various statues which include a bronze Fat Buddha, four-armed Vishnu, black stone-carved and jackal-faced Egyptian Anubis, a ceramic Christ on a wooden cross, and I believe the one in armour is supposed to be Sauron. I'm sure I blend right in. All is dark, mere silhouettes. Across from me is a wall dominated by a bookshelf. The library includes everything from advanced scientific texts to Garfield comics. The space between the statues and the bookshelf is all clutter. A massive wooden desk is covered in papers and books, along with knick-knacks, puzzles, and toys. Movie posters and surreal paintings cover any free space on the walls. There's no order, no feng-shui to the layout of the leather loveseat, record player, coffee table, and scattered chairs. I see two bongs, one glass and the other bamboo, and a few pipes. The dank smell of old marijuana smoke emanates from every surface. I wonder why Samuel would want this man for his grand project, but then I remember that Armand nurses the same habit.

The doorknob rattles. Keys jingle and lock turns. The door swings silently inward. A man enters his home, unaware that it has been breached. His blond hair and beard are shaggy. His brown, woollen, form-fitting zip-up sweater is an odd picture of neatness against his messy mane and abode. He hits the lights and I can see all the scattered details of his life. But, despite his big wide eyes, he doesn't yet see me sitting among his collection of carved gods and goddesses. I am silent and still. I observe Dustin Dobbs as he removes his blue backpack and tosses it on the couch. His face shows no emotion as he sits at his desk, chair squeaking slightly under his lean frame, mere feet from where I am watching him. He's a glorious deer, unaware of his hunter. The deer opens a drawer and pulls out a battered wooden box. Opens the lid and pulls out a jar filled with marijuana nuggets. He pops the jar and sticks his nose in, inhaling a big loud sniff of the green stuff.

"Aaahh," he says, and a big smile spreads across his face. Then he pulls out a few nuggets and puts them into a circular wooden grinder. The kind with all the little metal teeth inside to rip and tear the bud into a crumbly powder. I can already smell it, and I admit I appreciate the scent. Now he has a pile of dope on his desk. He gets up to put a record on, some weird electric organ music. He grabs his bong, taps the ash out of the chamber and replaces it. Stuffs the chamber with green goodness. Flicks his lighter, puts his mouth to the big opening, and breathes in until the transparent apparatus is filled with bubbling cloud.

I don't want to interrupt his peaceful ritual. I'm about to rip his life apart, so I let him have these final moments of peace. He removes the chamber and sucks all the smoke out of the tube so it's mostly clear again.

Then I speak.

"Dustin Dobbs!"

"Ahh!" he shrieks, arms flying up in the air.

His long bong twirls like a throwing knife, ejecting a spray of dirty water. He frantically tries to grab it but only succeeds in pushing it further away from him. It smashes on the floor, brackish bong water on polished hardwood, little black clots of resin.

"Ah man," he laments in a raspy voice, forgetting me already to grieve for his lost bong. Then his face whips back in my direction. "What the fuck, man? Who are you?"

"I'm either your best friend or your worst enemy," I say. I haven't moved from my perch. I expect that I can easily beat him to the door, and beat him into submission if necessary.

"That doesn't fucking explain much, man!" He fumbles in the drawer and pulls out a pencil, brandishing it like a knife. Then he hesitates, digs around some more, and pulls out a sharper compass.

"That won't help you," I tell him. "But I can. I believe you've met my brother?"

His eyes narrow. "Blackburn? I never met him personally, but I already told one of his messengers I'm not interested. Now he's sending family? I've got work to do at the university, and you're not going to have any fucking weed on fucking Mars!"

"I don't want you to go to Mars with my brother," I tell him in a steady voice. "I want you to help me kill him."

"Fuck that, man. I have nothing to do with this. Leave me out of whatever's going on."

I hold up a hand, from which dangles a set of steel handcuffs. "You're going to help whether you want to or not. But it will be much easier for everybody if you cooperate."

He hesitates, glaring at me, and I can see in his eyes that he's about to run. And then he does, pushing his chair at me and leaping over his broken bong in a graceless lunge. Of course I'm faster than him. I vault over the desk and make it to the exit. But he wasn't headed to the exit! He's gone into his kitchen, where I assume he'll grab some awkward weapon that I'll have to wrestle from him.

Three strides and I smash open the wooden door to his kitchen, just in time to see something flying through the air toward my face. I duck and a small bottle smashes against the door above me. Glass sprinkles my jacket and I hear a sizzling sound. "Did you throw acid at me?"

He laughs like a maniac and hurls another bottle. I run from the kitchen and rip off my jacket before the liquid can get through to my skin. I don't know how many bottles of that stuff he has, though he can't have much. "So it's a standoff!" I shout through the door.

"I have an infinite supply!" he shouts back ridiculously.

I go to his bookshelf and grab a copy of the Bible. I get his lighter from the desk, fan open the thin pages, and set it on fire. Then I kick open the door and throw the flaming book into the room. "You don't have an infinite supply of books," I yell. The record player is still oozing weird organ noises, so I pick up the record and snap it in half. "I'll wreck all your stuff and burn everything in this apartment."

"I'm not helping you kill anybody," he yells.

"He will kidnap you and take you to Mars, unless I help you," I say. "And not just you. He murdered my employees, wrecked my property. He even kidnapped my daughter!"

Silence. Then the door creaks open and his head appears, eyes peering at me, trying to find out if I'm lying. "You serious?"

I don't attack him. I don't yell. Maybe he'll listen to reason. So I just nod. "Our father is a vicious rat. I was strong enough to escape his ugliness, but my younger brother grew up just like him. Hateful and twisted. I'm trying to build a community, a place of health and learning, but my jealous brother has been ripping it apart."

"Is your community on Mars, too?"

"Africa."

"You think his Mars thing will work?"

"Fuck, no!" I bark. "Not when his whole plan is motivated by spite. He's stolen the right technology, kidnapped or hired the right team, but what is their guiding light? What attitude is taking itself to the stars?"

"What kind of technology?" Dustin asks breathlessly.

"They grew some sort of spacecraft underwater," I tell him, recalling the reports from Stephanie's proselytized crew. Then I tell him about the anti-magnet thrusters, rocket-backpacks, and other discoveries that I barely understand.

"Is that how you found me?"

"I got hold of his files, and some of his former employees are working for my daughter now. You have a meeting this week with a colleague? Doctor Fife?"

Dustin nods. "Tomorrow afternoon."

"They're going to grab you then, since you wouldn't join him willingly. Just like they grabbed my daughter. But I need to use you as bait."

Dustin shakes his head, still peering through the door. "You got a fucked up family, man!"

I sit down in his leather loveseat. From the tone of his voice I can tell that a personal appeal will work better than force. "You have no idea. Motherless bastards, the products of violation. I spent my whole life trying to get away, trying to build something healthy. But they wormed their way back in, like an infection rotting away all my work. I'll crush them all, smear them into the dirt.

But I'm so sick of the blood. Sick of crushing people."

"Maybe he's hurting just like you," Dustin suggests in his light, raspy, chirping voice. "Maybe this is his way of trying to connect with his brother. If your dad's as bad as you say he is, your brother might not know any other way to reach out."

The truth in his words can only weaken my resolve. "Some kinds of evil and weakness need to be stomped out."

In Dustin's distant eyes I see sympathy for my murderous brother. I can't afford to have compassion during wartime. But when I look at Dustin, the man whose home I invaded, all I can see is one more victim of the Blackburns. One more violation. I intend to use him, at his own risk, with or without his consent. Is this why I built Agartha?

"The choice is yours," I say. "I won't force you to help. If you ask me to leave, I'll leave you to your own devices, though my brother will try to take you as another scientist-slave." Even as I offer him his freedom I curse my own weakness. Am I getting soft? Whither, iron fist? Simultaneously, I wonder if I even mean it. If he asks me to leave, will I really leave?

Indeed, I will.

"Dude," Dustin says, stepping over where the

acid is burning indentations into the floor. "I'm sorry I threw acid at you. I'll help you catch this fucker."

Chapter 15

I am observing an outdoor eatery. With its wrought-iron chairs, cobbled patio, and the carved-stone facade of the restaurant, this eatery attempts to recreate the feeling of a Paris cafe, but it's walled in by American skyscrapers and cars. Similarly, hiding up here in a grimy parking garage and observing my baited trap via binoculars, I'm trying to recreate the silent patience of a camouflaged hunter in this urban jungle.

The traitor Doctor Fife is a fat slob. He sits with Dustin at a table in the very centre of the busy eatery, laughing and joking with his old colleague. Through the microphone Dustin agreed to wear I can hear every presumptuous compliment, every reminiscent anecdote. I can also hear the strain in Dustin's voice as he responds. The strain is not from fear, but his obvious inability to contain his disgust at the old friend who he now knows has sold him out to Samuel Blackburn. Fife blathers on oblivious to the fact that Dustin knows what's coming, and has agreed to be kidnapped so that I may get my clutches on my own traitor.

The stone patio is a large square, bustling with lunchtime patrons beneath the hot southern sun. The cafe building's huge glass panels set into elegant stone run across the west side of the patio, and a slow-moving four-lane downtown street covers the east side. North and south have pretty little gardens of dwarf trees and various-coloured flowers, leading up to office-buildings and parking garages.

By now Samuel must know that his Antarctica base has been conquered, but I'm hoping he believes his minions to have been butchered rather than recruited. He may not know how much I know about his plans. Will he still follow through with this planned kidnapping? Will he risk showing his face today?

A lone police car pulls up in front of the patio. Two men get out, dressed in crisp blue uniforms. I try to get a good look at their faces with my binoculars. Though their features are obscured by cap and shades, I recognize the one with black hair. I recognize Samuel Saffron, the book-keeper from Jasserty Salvage, his pale face and little smirk. I had him in my clutches. I laughed at his jokes. I merely stole his paperwork and his salvaged Scotch when, if I had known who he was, I could have stolen his very life. How could I not recognize the relevance of the pseudonym he'd chosen? Saffron, so expensive and delicate, to beat out rugged and cheaper Cinnamon. The prince was playing the pauper.

Dustin's back is to the road and he doesn't see the fake cops. But fat Doctor Fife sees with fidgety eyes, glancing from predator to prey twice before spreading an even wider smile to brute-force a final moment of extra trust from his mark. It doesn't work, of course. Dustin sees the nervous meaning in his betrayer's eyes and simply groans into the microphone. He slams back the rest of his gin and tonic just before he is flanked by the two cops.

Muffled, I hear Samuel's demand: "Mr. Dobbs, would you come with me please?"

I've instructed Dustin to submit to the false arrest, so that me and my small team may pursue and rescue him, taking hold of my brother in the process. But this is not what Dustin chooses to do.

He slams his fist on the metal table in an obviously-exaggerated and uncharacteristically rebellious display of frustration. "It's *Doctor Dobbs*, officer!"

Samuel grimaces. "Of course. Now, Dr. Dobbs, we have some questions we'd like to ask you. So, if you please?"

He pounds the table again. "What exactly is this about?"

The other cop, a muscle-bound, bald and

tanned man, puts his hand on Dustin's shoulder. I have no way of communicating with my bait, no way to tell him to calm the fuck down and let them take him. No way to prevent him, when he flips the table onto his fat and blubbering Judas, and runs into the crowd screaming, "Fucking pigs!"

Samuel is clearly not a man of physical action. He frowns uselessly at his escaping prey. But his partner is quicker and stronger. "On the ground!" he bellows, feet pounding the patio stones like he was built to run. In no time he's tackled Dustin, who struggles feebly, and binds his hands in cuffs. Hauls him to his feet and shoves him stumbling toward the cop car. Doors slam. The car drives away.

"Cop car heading south with Samuel and Dustin inside!" I tell the team through the mic clipped to my collar before donning a brown motorcycle helmet. My binoculars go in a fanny pack and my ass goes on the matte-brown sportsbike beside me. When I rev the engine it doesn't quite roar but it's more than a purr. The parking garage has an exit to the street where the cop car is just rolling past. In the drivers seat Samuel looks right at me but gives no sign of recognition. A minivan follows right behind him and I don't know if they're part of his team. I pull out behind the van and follow at a safe distance.

Ahead and behind I spy two brown bikes identical to mine, driven by identically brown-clad motorists. Members of Stephanie's new team, helping me turn against their old master. They zip past on the perpendicular streets surrounding us. I know there are three more nearby, ready to follow Samuel's path using erratic criss-crossing patterns and reporting his location and direction via headsets. Only five of them, plus myself, have experience with sportbikes. Armand will follow somewhere behind in a sedan, ready to transport prisoners once we capture them. Felix and Stephanie are nearby in a helicopter as backup.

"East down O'Connor Street," I say when Samuel's car turns. I Keep going straight, so as not to be seen following. But I take the next left, where skyscrapers have very suddenly been replaced with a neighbourhood of old brick houses, the front yards bursting with professionally-maintained greenery and flowers. When someone's voice speaks in my ear, "South down Charlemagne Lane," I turn right down Bristol, which is one street past them. Slow down. I want to maintain a slight lead, so we keep them surrounded, but I can't get too far ahead for the next time they turn.

Every time I have to stop at a red light or stop sign I feel the jitters. Will we lose him? "Who has eyes on him?" I say into the mic.

Nobody answers. So I get onto Charlemagne

and look up and down for the cop car. Nowhere to be seen, so I go slowly in the direction they last spotted him. "Still no visual?" I ask. The silence from my team is deadening. "Armand can you hear me?"

"Yes," he says. "No visual Mr. Cinnamon."

"Number One?" I call. Each of the five bikers have been assigned a number for quick communication. I am Six.

Nobody answers.

"Number Two?" I enquire.

"I'm here," a man answers back. "But I can't find the cop car. I criss-crossed Charlemagne three times, but no visual."

"Number Three?"

"No visual," Number Three grunts.

"Four?" I snap.

"I think somebody's following me," Number Four responds. "Someone on a yellow bike, tailing me for at least a few blocks."

"Lose him," I say. "Number Five?"

"I see a cop car going into a parking garage on Smythe and Keeling," she says. It's the Bitch. "I can't tell if it's them or not. Should I follow?"

"Go around the block once and then head in. Everybody else follow Five. Armand keep the motor running by the exit."

Two more turns and a few more blocks and I emerge from the tree-covered quaintness of the high-end brick-home suburb. I spy a parking garage beside the cement megalith of an on-ramp leading to the raised freeway. The grey pillars and sprawl of branching roadways dwarf the sturdy little multi-level building into which two brown motorcycles disappear. I follow them into the first floor of the garage, just in time to see them head up to the second. The fourth floor would be the roof, but we don't make it that far. The cop car has pulled into a spot in the centre of the third level.

Samuel and his partner have already exited the cop car. They're parked in an open area of several empty spaces. Sam has unlocked a nearby green Honda Civic and is changing into slacks and a brown turtleneck sweater. His partner, still dressed like a cop, is pulling an uncooperative Dustin out of the back seat. "Surround them. Let's get them while they're switching cars," I say softly.

Motorcycle engines echo off the cement and parked cars. Another bike follows behind me. There should be six bikes, but only four of us arrive in time to flank the three men. We stop our vehicles together, two of us in each aisle surrounding them.

"Julius!" Samuel shouts in surprise as soon as he sees the bikes, even though I haven't removed my helmet. They know what's up. His partner leaves off from Dustin and whips out a gun. One of my brown bikers is faster, aiming a tiny pistol which cracks off four sharp shots. The fake cop groans and falls to his knees as the echoes of the gun's report shame him with reverberating reminders of the cause of his pain. He's not dead, but the four growing red spots on his chest demand medical attention that he may never receive.

Samuel runs around to the other side of the Civic to open the drivers' side door. I'm already there before he can slam it shut. I grab the loose, thick fabric of the brown sweater and haul him out, hurling him face-first into the siding of the black car parked beside us.

Crumpled on the floor. Nose bleeding. "Goddammit," he grunts, and I stomp on his hand with my boot. He's not a strong man. Doesn't know how to fight. I haul him up and throw him over the hood of the Civic, and he tumbles onto the open pavement. He manages to get to his feet before I get around the car, taking off my helmet and tossing it aside. I smile as I watch him prepare to take a swing at me. It's a big, wide-flying fist. I hop back so his swing goes too far. He stumbles again, and I drive my fist into his stomach. Then throw him against the car again, where he collapses, clutching his guts and panting.

The others have retrieved the keys for Dustin's handcuffs from Samuel's bleeding partner. They toss the keys to Dustin, who can now fumble to free himself within the back seat of the cop car.

I crouch before my brother, elbow on knee and chin in hand as I study him. "Wretched fellow-progeny," I say. "Was it nature or nurture? What turned you into a fratricidal deviant?"

Smirking Samuel looks past me and points at Dustin, who is still trying to remove his own handcuffs. "The last piece of my puzzle, and you stole him away, big brother!"

"You did the same to me," I remind him. "Why not just build your own empire? What compelled you to cannibalize mine?"

The light in his eyes and the snarl on his lips tell me more than his words. Now he is searching me, frightened of me, hateful and curious. But he gives a flippant shrug and looks away as he answers. "Why start from scratch when I could just take what you built and use it for something better?"

The Bitch speaks in my ear. "No time to talk. Kill him or cuff him, but we gotta go."

Despite my purpose and my rage I long to reach out to this wretched fool. I want to understand him, and to share with him the inner glory that I learned to grasp. I know he has been crippled by our father's cruelty, shaded in that darkness. My heart is twisted in a knot by the paradox: he does not want my help, he does not seek my friendship, and because of these things I feel the responsibility to give him these gifts.

Time for all that later. I turn around and look at Dustin. "Did you get those handcuffs off?"

Still in the back seat of the cop car with the door open, he dangles the chains with a big smile.

"Throw them to me!"

As he bends his arm for the throw, something skitters across the pavement. Round, green, and metal, it clatters and bounces. The grenade comes to a stop beneath the cop car.

"Dustin get out!"

There is no fireball and barely a flash of light, but the cracking boom is immense in this enclosed space and the car is lifted into the air as chunks of metal and glass fly. A shard of smoking steel embeds itself sharply in the siding of the green Civic. Other pieces twirl and scratch across the pavement. A second explosion follows, either from a second grenade or something ignited by the first, but this one splits the car in half. An arm flies over my head, clothed in brown wool.

I hear the engine of a sportbike. More of my crew must be arriving.

"Where did those grenades come from?" I say.

"No idea," comes the response.

The parking garage is open-air, every floor looking out on the world below. A man climbs over the railing. Red hair and very serious. He has a grenade in one hand and a knife in the other. "I'm gonna gut you like you gutted Alex," Gavin says, and tosses the grenade toward my bikers. They scatter, but the explosion destroys one of their bikes and sends a brown-suited body flying head over foot, to land with a horrible, screaming, bone-breaking thud against a pickup truck whose car alarm begins to cry.

Someone arrives on a yellow bike and red helmet, brakes and palms a pistol. One of my bikers laying on the ground gets a torso full of bullets. I'm close enough to jump him and knock the fucker off his bike. His red helmet protects his face but nothing can prevent me from pinning him to the ground, face down. I clamp down on his his right arm, pull back against the elbow until it breaks. He's writhing and making noises louder than his bike. I break his other arm and steal his gun, turning around to look for Gavin.

The Bitch has her helmet off. She's wrestling with my Scottish opponent, and I find that I'm jealous. He kicks her off and jumps to his feet, brandishing his knife. I look at the Bitch. "We can take him together," I say.

"Samuel's driving away," she reminds me. "You follow him, I'll take care of this snowflake."

It's true. The green Honda is already disappearing down the exit ramp. I commandeer the yellow sportbike and leave them to their battle.

My plan is ruined. My team is dismantled. But the mission has not yet failed. I can still capture Samuel and set things straight for the future.

The Civic bounces out onto the street, forcing an oncoming car to swerve as Samuel bullishly merges with traffic. Merge? No. He's weaving between cars and breaking the speed limit. Well, none of the Blackburns were ever much for the law. My bike's engines are like a mosquito mixed with a lion. I weave easier through the traffic on my little crotch-rocket, keeping up with my brother with less effort. He breaks into the opposing lane to pass a delivery truck on the left, but I slide slickly between the truck and a taxi. He turns left, the bastard, and I've got to come to a screeching stop, almost losing balance as the tires scratch out a puff of black smoke across the pavement. Reverse direction. Catch up on the next street.

Somebody else has caught up too. As we pass an old inner-city cemetery I see the bike that's just begun to follow me. It's one of our brown bikes. I can't see Gavin's red hair underneath the stolen brown helmet, but you can't miss his green jumpsuit. He's gunning for me hard, motor roaring, taking every risk as he dodges every high-velocity chunk of metal between us.

Can I keep up with Samuel while Gavin's chasing me down? Where are the rest of my team? He's right on my tail. A dangerous stunt, I pull my pistol and take a shot behind me. No time to aim. I put a hole in the pavement but Gavin backs off. Re-holster the weapon. Both hands back to steering now before I begin to wobble.

Samuel speeds up at the sound of the gun, bursting ahead just after a yellow light turns red and oblivious pedestrians have begin to walk. I hear a sickening thump and somebody scream. My bike follows in the Civic's wake as the sea of shocked people parts, but I whizz past the broken bodies of two hapless victims of Samuel's rampaging flight from justice.

Gavin reaches for me from the right. I veer into oncoming traffic, barely missing a yellow Mustang as I pass in front of it, and stay on the white line as a terrifying array of vehicles whip past me on each side. Mere inches exist between me and each passing vehicle. The wind shakes my body but the bike sticks tight to the road. It's a great relief when this cluster of cars ends and I can escape into the proper stream.

Now Gavin has a friend. Red bike, red suit, red helmet, they are a drop of blood pumped through the three lanes of urban artery. They seek me and I evade. No weapons are drawn. They just aim themselves at me, seeking to knock me into traffic. So I speed up, slow down, slide dangerously left and right as people honk at our irresponsible driving.

This strip has major traffic lights on every block and more pedestrians barely escape with their lives as Samuel smashes through another red light. I follow with Gavin right beside me and the red bike somewhere close behind. Heavy traffic and a commercial area lay ahead. Vast construction approaches on the left. With all those lights, all those cars and walkers, Samuel is sure to kill some strangers in his frenzy to escape, and my hard-driving chase is only spurring him on. Plus I have Gavin to deal with. Should I break off from my pursuit of the traitorous brother to deal with the bereaved one?

Am I getting soft? Tempering my will for the sake of strangers' lives? No time to be indecisive. And Gavin deserves his confrontation. I turn left, cutting across traffic and in between the great chain-link fence gates which mark the line where pavement turns to gravel. I race in with too much speed. The rough terrain threatens to topple my bike, yet I gun the engine and burst ahead full-throttle. Past a dump truck carrying a full load of dirt, beneath a crane lifting a shipping container up to the roof of the metal framework of a many-storied building. Teams of men in reflective vests and yellow hardhats are all oblivious to the three bikes that have torn into their midst.

I see an opportunity. The pieces have lined

up too perfectly for me to ignore. Can I survive it? Will Gavin take the dangerous bait?

I aim with max-speed violence at a pile of gravel. The front wheel hits the edge of the hill, shaking my whole frame as my aching arms loudly absorb an unhealthy amount of the bike's forward momentum. The back wheel hits immediately after and I go charging up the hill, spurting rocks and dirt in a cloud behind me as my wheels drag me up and up toward the peak of this artificial mound. Still revving, accelerating again, I reach the top and fly into the air in an arc of helplessness. I look behind me and see Gavin flying even higher. His red-bike companion seems to have wobbled before soaring. He can't get the same height, and didn't aim well. He smashes into a low brick building with a crack and a thud, leaving Gavin and I to finish the battle.

Why did I drive my motor bike up the hill and into the sky? Because here comes the crane lifting its shipping container, right in my path. Well, almost right in my path. The bike has risen but now gravity is bringing her down, and me with her. Like a fool I thought I could jump the bike right through the open door. A dreadful space exists between my tires and the tiny construction equipment below.

So I leap. Abandoning Yoshi. My feet shove off from the bike, pushing her down and giving me a tiny boost up, up, and my fingers grasp the dirty ledge of the shipping container. I dangle like a Christmas ornament. Like a booger. Gavin's bike goes flying above me and I hear it loudly land on the top of the container. Then, after a short clattering noise, I see it fall off the other side. But Gavin doesn't fall with it.

I haul myself up and inside the box. It's packed with equipment from bound bales of heavy metal bars to large table saws, tall toolboxes, locked chests and drawers. It's all strapped in. The great bulk of gear sticks out of the opening so much that they opted to remove the doors. I climb in, looking for something to use as a weapon.

A shadow covers me and I dodge behind a box just as a small knife flits through the space where I just stood. I peek my head out and see the sparkle of Gavin's eyes, and the glint of his blades. "You're trapped," he calmly observes.

"So are you," I remind him. It's not like he can safely escape out the open door when we're so far up in the air. I'm looking for anything that's not tied down, so I can deflect his attacks and beat him to death. But the construction workers didn't want anything moving around in-transit, so any piece of metal I get my hands on is restricted by hard steel straps.

But what's in these drawers beneath the table saw? They're not locked, just latched. I press the buttons and haul out the drawer. Inside I discover an unprecedented bounty of glorious death. Circular saws, fresh blades, weaponized frisbees. A dozen of them are nestled snugly in little slots like vinyl records.

I grip one in each hand, and I stand to face my tormentor.

He's come closer than I thought. He's almost in arms-reach, gripping a pistol and a big, bloody knife. I wonder where the blood came from, and I remember how I left the Bitch to fight him. My arm is moving before I finish standing. The metal frisbee makes a satisfying whirring sound as it cuts the air between me and my target. Gavin's response is automatic. His knife comes up to protect his face even as he dodges to the right. The metal teeth of the spinning saw grab the knife's blade and rip it from his grip, flinging it out into the bright blue sky behind him. The disc is free now, flying like a bird on the breeze. I hope it doesn't hit anybody when it falls.

He aims his pistol, but I've already throw the second disc. We must both be exceptional shots. He pulls the trigger and the retort is echoed and amplified against these metal walls. My saw blade explodes into a dozen pieces when the bullet hits it.

I duck down and hide again before he can pull the trigger some more. Two more blades are in my hands, but I've lost the element of surprise. I've brought circular saws to a gun-fight.

"I'm gonna show you your own guts," Gavin reminds me. "I don't care about winning anymore. I don't want Agartha, I don't want money, and I don't want to help Samuel get to Mars. You took my brother, and you can't give him back. We're locked in, Julius. It's just you and me."

"It's not just you and me," I tell him. "There are seven billion people, and the dream of Agartha is my gift to them all."

"I don't think there's room in that little volcano for all of them."

"You lack imagination," I tell him. "That's why you lost your brother, and that's why you'll lose again today."

I make my risky move. I've done some quick mental calculations based on my knowledge of billiards, replacing balls with discs, and replacing the 2D tabletop with this 3D space. From the relative safety of my hiding spot I throw a blade underhand spinning up at the ceiling. My biggest fear is that it will stick into the metal.

It bounces just as I stand again. Gavin would like to shoot at the easy target I've provided him, but the saw is bouncing right at his head, and he has to dodge. As he evades one blade I throw two more. I'm not aiming high for a kill. I aim low to maim.

The bouncing blade sinks into the plywood floor with a THUNK sound. The second one shreds the leather of his boot but gets stuck in the steel toe which saves his foot from dismemberment. My third blade slams into his pistol and knocks it out of his hand. They both go bouncing out the door to rain down on the construction site.

I duck again to grab two more blades. Gavin has retrieved his own from boot and board. We face each other like cowboys in this duel-to-the-death. Who will draw first? Who will die?

He throws first, and aims for my guts. I'm sure that in his mind's eye he sees my intestines shredded and spilling before he finally cuts my throat. But my reflexes serve me well. I buckle and bend so my torso evades the slice, and with the same movement my right arm launches its prize.

Gavin's reflexes are even faster than mine! He instinctively catches the blade and it cuts off his whole hand above the thumb before his brain can even register the mistake that it made. The blood pours out like somebody's squeezing a ketchup container, and he throws his other blade right at my head.

I punch it out of the air, hitting the side instead of the front of course, and it clatters among the equipment. Now I know I've won because I've still got a weapon and he has none, plus he's missing a hand. Still, no time to get cocky. I aim for his throat. He shifts to one side and the blade catches his upper arm, rips the flesh and breaks the bone. Now his arm is hanging by raggedly exposed muscle. But his other hand is his good hand and with it he grimly grabs the weapon.

The tables have turned. I duck and grab two more blades. As I stand, he throws his weapon with desperate power and speed. I deflect it with the blade in my left hand. It tears my skin and rips the metal disc from my grip. But I'm already throwing with my right.

It lands in his chest. Perfectly vertical, right in his sternum. It sinks a full half-way in before it stops. He stumbles backward with a wheezing gasp. His good hand fumbles for the blade. Does he still think he can fight? Let's cure him of that delusion!

I pick up two of the closest discarded blades, and hurl them at my weakened enemy. The first one he tries to catch again, like a fool, and loses his whole good hand. Morbidly, hand and blade tumble out the door. My next and final throw ends it all. It hits him vertically right above the nose and splits his face and head in half. It looks like a poorly-placed mohawk. He stumbles for a moment, but there isn't much distance in here to stumble before the floor disappears. And Gavin disappears with it, falling out and down to the hard dirt far below.

You've had your confrontation, Gavin. It didn't turn out as you intended.

My troubles aren't over. I hear sirens.

I peek over the edge and see that the crane has stopped moving. Cop cars have arrived on the scene and are taking over the construction site far below. I see Gavin's corpse with a few boys in blue studying him. I expect they'll bring the crane down, with me in the box to arrest me.

Luckily they've stopped the crane just above ledge of the building where this shipping container was to be delivered. And they have not yet seen my face.

The door still dangles over space, but the backend of the shipping container is above the building's roof. I grab a bundle of rope from the back, climb atop the container, and walk to the other end. The breeze rustles my beard. I can't hear what they're shouting below. I leap down onto the roof and land hard on the cement. The impact shakes my bones and guts, and I have to rest for a moment. But nothing is broken, so I continue to the other side of the building. I climb scaffolding down to the ground, where I scale the fence and exit the construction site unseen.

My team is long-gone and I've lost all means of communication. I look in the sky for Felix's helicopter, but see only pastel blue and pretty clouds. I scan the roads for Armand's black sedan, and there it is! I scream his name and he does a quick u-turn to pick me up.

"I've been circling the block since you drove into the construction site," he tells me as we drive out of the city.

"Where is everybody?" I ask. "Where is my brother?"

"The whole team is all Stephanie's crew," Armand reminds me. "Except for me and you. They are chasing your brother, and ignoring my communications. I believe she wants to do this without her father, Mr. Cinnamon."

"Well if she wants to catch him without me, she'll have to do it before we catch up."

Armand is grinning. The car smells like weed. "I think we know where they have gone."

Chapter 16

The tree-leaves are agitated by a slow breeze as we zoom past them on the lonely highway. Are they waving me on for my victory lap? Or shaking their fists at a fool who's let everything fall apart? On Armand's radio I try to entice my daughter to speak to me but she's either out of range or ignoring me. Armand pushes his car's engines to their limits en route to Mother Ocean.

"I don't know what you're planning,

Stephanie," I speak into the handheld black radio mic, tuned to the previously-agreed-upon frequency, "but there's power in numbers! I don't know if he's killed you, if you're betraying me, or if you're just not listening. You gain nothing by cutting me out, and now I'm driving in with no information. We must coordinate. Talk to me!"

We listen for a response, but the only noises are the surging of the engine and occasional cars whooshing past in the opposite lane. The frustrating silence grinds my teeth and snarls my lip. Armand is driving and my daughter is fighting Samuel, and all I can do is sit here in the passenger seat like a child.

"Stephanie," I tell the mic. "If you're fighting him without me, you're a fool abandoning her most dangerous weapon. If you defeat him and take his ship to Mars, you'll be taking a fool's equipment on a doomed errand. Work with me! *Talk to me god-dammit!*"

Armand turns off the highway. We crest the final hill which leads us down the slope toward the ocean which spreads out before us. Just below are the lonely docks, the shack where I'd stolen the motorboat and rode out for my underwater adventure. But now there is a new, dark fixture out in the water.

Four black spires are rising up from the ocean depths, and I recognize them. Wait, I recognize them twice! They are the looming towers of blackness which surrounded my battery when I discovered it underwater. And lo, here is the battery itself emerging from the water! I can see the features of the spires more clearly now that they're exposed to the clear sunlight. This is a distorted replica of Castle Blackburn, dripping with ocean water as it floats higher. The stones are not the rough rectangles of my father's abode, but weird jagged shapes. The spires too are not straight but crooked. My ultimate battery has been built into the top of this abomination. This seems to contradict what Samuel's crew told Stephanie in Antarctica. I thought Samuel's plans were clear: he was supposed to be growing a spaceship underwater with weird stolen nanotech, powered by my battery. But this castle is no spaceship.

The radio speaks.

"Don't follow us, Daddy," my daughter's static-ridden voice tells me. She's so matter-of-fact, so dark and confident. "I'm stealing Mars from Uncle Sammy. He has his space-castle, scientists, your battery, and everything we need to start a colony. I'll take it all from him like he tried to take it from you. The Rasskakovs and Cinnamons will be the first rulers of a new planet, but you have to stay here and take care of Agartha. This is my mess and I'm cleaning it up. But now I have an empire, too. And I'm keeping your big battery."

"Let me help!" I demand. "Where are you?"

She responds, but it's all static. They're out of range, or something is blocking the signal.

The castle is out of the water completely now. It floats and flies upwards on some invisible stolen technology. The black shape is beautiful against the green ocean and blue sky. But it's not alone in its ascent. Great glass pods orbit around it, the ones I'd seen underwater before getting netted. Is that a cluster of flies? No, it's men and women wearing rocket-packs, battling in the skies and seeking entry to the elevating fortress.

Several corpses float in the water by the docks, human driftwood rocking in the turbulent afterwaves of the launched spacecraft. A couple more dot the docks. There has been a battle. Some of the dead wear the black uniforms of Samuel's crew, while others are Stephanie's brown-clad recruits.

Someone's not dead. On the wooden slabs leading to the shack I recognize the blond hair and sturdy frame of the Bitch. There's a thick white bandage wrapped around one leg. The castle has eclipsed the sun just above her head, surrounded by its cluster of pods and people. Armand parks the car and I step out. "She left her best man behind?"

The Bitch crosses her arms. "I'm on a special

mission," she says.

"You shouldn't be down here when Stephanie needs help taking the castle!" I tell her. "Are there more jet-packs?"

She nods with a grin and jerks her thumb behind her to the shack. "There's a few more in there! But that's why I'm here. See, Stephanie's afraid you're going to follow her to Mars, and then who will take care of Agartha? Earth is yours, but Mars belongs to my Ice Queen. She'll kill Samuel for you, but she doesn't want you getting in the way and causing shit."

"Causing shit?" I growl. "This was all going smoothly when I was in control. You've been the boss bitch for two of my family members who have unravelled years of hard work. Straighten out your crooked brain and join Armand and me. Get us some rocket-packs, fly with us up to the castle so we can make sure she wins!"

"I got orders," she says, relishing the confrontation. "I'll follow her up there, once you're tied up down here."

Armand steps beside me. "This will not happen, woman. We are following Miss Stephanie."

"The rockets are in the shack, if you can get past me!"

Armand and I march in step. I keep a close eye to make sure she doesn't pull a gun, though I doubt she'll kill either of us if she's loyal to

Stephanie. Two strong men should be able to overpower this smirking lackey.

The Bitch un-crosses her arms and adopts a wide-legged fighting pose. I can see the spring in her step, her readiness to engage the enemy. Her hand flashes out to strike Armand's head but he easily catches her wrist. That's when I see what was in her hand: A can of pepper-spray, which she now sprays down over his sunglasses, before kicking him in the balls.

It's been a long time since I've seen Armand lose control, but the animal rage in his warlike scream transforms us all to basic primates. He brings his fists down on her shoulders, slamming her onto her knees which make a heavy clunk against the wood of the dock. The pepper-spray goes flying across the boards, under the rusted metal railing to plop in the ocean. Armand turns aside to nurse his burning eyes and I leap on the fallen ogre. She's fast and rolls to throw me over her, but I keep hold of her arm and we wind up grappling. Now I'm on top of her, seeking a hold. But she worms out, wraps her legs around to push me down on my back, and then mounts me. As I try to get a leg up to push her off, she snaps a handcuff on my right wrist.

With my overpowering strength I get her down onto her side, but her feminine flexibility slips like a snake out of every move I make. Her body rubs against mine. She pants with exertion. She may be strong but she's still a woman, and the feeling of her feminine form pushing against mine, her breath exploding from her heaving chest, the grinding of her hips as she straddles and dominates me with her legs, all conspire to agitate my desire. I'm focused to the point of obsession, but a woman's breath is a magic spell. When she feels me harden against her she pushes against it, seeking to distract and weaken me.

We each seek bone-breaking holds but neither succeeds in total domination. My surging manhood, forming a great tent in my brown pants, pushes against the Bitch as I struggle for a rear hold which she frustratingly escapes. We slide over each other like a blob of oil and water floating in space, drawn together by gravity, unable to truly mix, rocked with waves of seismic power. Somehow her elbow finds my face once, twice, and the third strike smashes my already-broken nose. A flurry of activity, a blitzkrieg of arms and legs, and now she's snapped the other cuff to the rusted metal railing of the docks.

"You think you've won?" I growl. "I'll rip my fucking hand off and follow my daughter anyway. You're just weakening her greatest ally!"

But she's not paying attention to my words, nor is she prudently backing away from her chained opponent. I'm sitting on the dock with my back against the railing, right hand chained, and she's still straddling me, rubbing her crotch against mine. Her right hand grips my free left wrist, which I'm trying to manoeuvre to push her off. The physical friction feels fucking good, and merry thoughts dance in my head of all the things I'd like to do with this beast of a woman. But I'm a busy man, a man on a mission, and I don't have time for this shit. With every second the castle flies further away.

"Get off me, woman!" I command.

"You're mine," she whispers in my ear. "My prize!"

Her tits, bulging to be free from the confines of her shirt, rub against my face. I feel a set of keys in the breast pocket. With her left hand she reaches down to unbutton my pants, and pulls out my iron tower so it can taste the salty air. She holds it for a moment in her hand, getting a feel for every ripple and vein. I pull back, torn in half by rage and desire. She lets go of my cock and grabs onto her pussy, caressing herself roughly through the fabric. Her hand balls into a fist gripping a handful of her pant-cloth, and with a slow and steady ripping sound she tears her own pants off. She performs the same motion with her elastic sports underwear, and I behold her smooth thighs leading up to her blond muff. My nose flares and drinks up the woman-sex scent which overpowers that of the nearby ocean.

My traitorous hard-on reaches up toward the tangled forest which hovers above it even as I pull my hips back as far as they can go. I swear I can see her hole from here, opening and closing like the mouth of a hungry little fish as she lowers herself toward her prize. It hungrily drools a sticky drop onto my red tip. I move left and right, trying to avoid the sweet inevitable. But the searching fish-mouth takes a bite of the strawberry, and swallows it whole. Wet friction pulls the skin of my manhood taut inside the tight confines of her secret tunnel as she lowers herself, impales herself upon me. My shaft is too long and she can't take anymore, and yet she pushes down, crumpling me inside her. Then she pulls up, slowly, until only the tip is just barely still inside. Down she comes again, harder and clenching. Faster now she pumps me, finding her own rhythm and trying different angles to stimulate herself. My willpower finally dissolves and my body responds to her rhythm.

She guides my free hand to her ass where I feel hard muscle below plump flesh. I clamp on, take charge, and begin to pump her from below. She throws her head back like a wolf howling at the moon. Pump, pound, slam. I grunt and ram myself deeper with each brutal thrust. She arches her back so far I fear she'll break in half.

She puts both her hands on the ground and

positions herself for sexual climax. I reach up to grab her tit. I massage the beautiful softness, right where those keys are nestled, just as she begins to shudder. My hand squeezes tighter and tighter, I pump harder and harder. Her voice breaks out a noise that alternates between wailing and grunting as I rip the pocket off of her shirt. Now my toes curls, my head explodes with light, and I feel my genes shoot up into her womb in a series of shuddering volcanic gushes.

She collapses off of me, and I unlock my cuffs with the key I just stole. There's a wet spot darkening the dock where our mixed juices have leaked. There's also blood on the docks from the ugly wound on her outer thigh, bleeding through its bandage. I remember Gavin's bloody knife.

I tuck my satisfied and softening junk back into my pants and look at Armand, who seems to have recovered from his pepper-spray attack. "You just stood there while she raped me," I accuse.

"You were asking for it, Mr. Cinnamon," he replies with a grin. "But while you seduced the lady I gathered the rockets from the shack, and weapons from the car. Shall we storm the castle?"

The massive castle is the size of a fingernail to the left of the sun as we strap into the heavy contraptions that Armand has dragged out. The rocket-backpacks are red and white, and it hurts my knees and back to lift their weight on my shoulders. I grip the pods which extend from the chest-piece on their little metal cords. Don a brown helmet. Stand back on the beach. Press both buttons, and the weight on my shoulders disappears.

Also disappearing is the land below, the Bitch who covers her satisfied sex with one hand, the beach which becomes a thin beige strip. I stop looking down and start looking up. Wind batters my face. Where is the castle? Where is the black dungeon in the sky? Ah, there it is! Contrasted against a cloud. I expected hot fire to explode from the rockets but instead it's a cold blast of gas. I test the controls. Squeezing deeper on the large buttons can shift me left or right. Smaller buttons activate secondary jets to nudge me up or down. It's an awkward ride. I'm no rocketeer! But through criss-crossing trajectories I manage to aim generally at my target.

The black spot takes a more distinctive form as I accelerate closer and closer. Contained in that blackness is a twisted emotional knot. My beloved daughter, the only person for whom I would sacrifice all my power, who has thrown wrenches into the gears of that very power. And my wretched brother, who has risked so much just to make me suffer and decay. Wisps of cloud rush by, ghostly sentinels of Heaven, and I realize that no

Earthly ambition has brought me here. My plans for Agartha will not be helped by this sky-bound excursion, unless I can get my battery back to Earth in one piece. Concern for my daughter is a motivator, yes. So is my lust for revenge. But the real power that propels me is the sheer gravity of that tangled knot. Stephanie has defeated Samuel before, and perhaps she can do it again. Then my progeny will be secure, and my revenge realized. And yet here I am, following her against her will, pulled in like a fool by that emotional knot. Not foolish for caring, but for believing my clumsy fingers could ever untie such a tangle. Should I turn back? Never. Not while there is still a chance that the foolish girl needs help.

What's my altitude? How far will this jetpack take me? And how will I gain entry to the castle once I catch up? All these questions become moot as the castle disappears into a continent-sized cloud. I soon follow it. Surrounded by misty white with no way to navigate. How will I know if I've flown too far? What's to prevent me from smashing suddenly into the stone walls?

Not to fear. A dark form appears ahead of me, the looming megalith. Its crooked towers send the mist swirling. But where are the pods that orbited it? And the other rocketeers who preceded me? I receive my answers in the order I asked them. A green glass pod glides over me, accompanied by an electronic warbling sound, and almost hits my jet pack. It barely misses, but the air is so disturbed that I go tumbling and swirling. I lose my direction, and just in time, for I see a body in a brown uniform fly through the trajectory I just lost. He has no jetpack, and something has gored his guts. More brown-clad corpses and pieces of corpses follow, tumbling in a rain representing the possibility of my daughter's failure. Where are they coming from? I adjust my course and blast faster through the clouds.

Shall I knock at the front door? No. Instead I aim left, away from the fortress. Then I turn a harder right to come at it from the side. If this replica is accurate I should be headed for my own old bedroom window. The black wall takes up my entire field of vision, and there indeed is my window. Its shape is melted and surreal, but the opening is wide enough. I realize, possibly too late, that this castle is headed for the vacuum of space, and the window won't simply be open for me to climb through. I see stained glass. As I rush toward it I pull a pistol and aim. Shot after shot bounces off the hard glass, and it's too late for me to turn away! The final bullet creates a solitary crack before my body rams into the pane. There is no light tinkling of shattered glass. Instead it's all hard clunks and the dull whine of the wind rushing in through the new opening. I've let go of the jets' thruster buttons, of course, but I still tumble all the way through my old room. I knock over a wooden shelf and the books go flying across the rug. Somehow I land face-up on the bed, which is bigger and softer than the one I slept on as a child.

There is a woman in my bed. Her shoulder-length brown hair is darker than her brown uniform. One of Stephanie's crew. She's curled up in the foetal position, clutching her gut and laying in a pool of blood. Her wound is too big for her two hands to cover.

"Julius," she gasps, and a thick gush of blood pours in a gurgling bubble from her lips.

I get out of the jetpack and check my own limbs for injuries. My body, and weapons, are intact. Fog pours in through the shattered window and I wonder where Armand is. A trail of blood leads from the bed to a tall bookshelf set against the wall.

"What happened?" I say to the wounded woman. "Where's Stephanie?"

"We lost," she gasps. "They killed all the men, and..."

"What? And what?"

She beckons for me to come closer, and I warily obey. A bloody hand clamps my shoulder and she says, "This whole place is a... sex dungeon!

We knew Samuel was stealing technology. He stole the anti-magnet wave-drive from the Chinese, and he stole your battery to power it and fly this castle. He stole the nanotech to grow this castle underwater, like he tried to steal your rock-eater nanobots. *But he was also stealing women!* There must be a hundred of them chained to the walls. They're..."

She coughs and a spatter of blood flecks my face, but I do not flinch from her dying monologue.

"They're so beautiful," she continues with a painful sigh. "The most beautiful women from around the world, kidnapped, and chained to the walls for Samuel's pleasure. And for his men. On Mars they'll be brood mares. Now they have..."

"Stephanie," I growl.

She nods. "And Stephanie's women."

"How did you escape?" I ask. "Where are the others?"

She points back along her trail of blood. "Tunnels... behind the bookcase... in every room. Stephanie is tied up, on display, hanging in the main hall."

I grip her hand. "Thank you. I'll free them all and take the castle for Stephanie."

Her eyes clamp tightly shut and she bites her bloody lip. "They'll catch you. They'll kill you like the killed the men. They're too strong. The... the..."

"The what?"

"Suits of armour," she breathes, and it's her

last breath. Her body goes limp. Warm blood still pours from her mangled gut, traitorous and shining as it escapes its dead host.

Suits of armour? I recall those metal hands that threw me out of my father's castle. Are they here in the new castle now? Or has he made replicas?

I take another look out the window to see if I can spot Armand, but no forms are visible through the thick fog that still pours in like a ghost.

How to open this bookshelf? I could destroy the dark stained wood, but I expect there's something harder behind the back panel. I see no buttons or levers. Some book perhaps? Which one would Samuel use as an entry to his sex-dungeon? I see one called "The Martian," and I give it a tug. The paperback comes out, but nothing happens. I toss it on the nearby dresser and search for another promising title. "Kane and Abel," by Jeffery Archer? I pull on the hardcover and meet resistance. I grip it tighter between my fingers and pull hard. A satisfying rumble shakes the rocky walls, like heavy machinery lumbering to life. A hiss of escaping gas. The shelf swings out quietly on well oiled and well hidden hinges. A steady warm breeze contrasts with the cooling air of the room, stirring up the cloudy influx like milk in coffee.

A steep spiral staircase descends before me.

The steps are irregular in slant and height, the stones of the wall the same jagged puzzle pieces of the room behind me and the great walls outside. Some flickering light reaches up like flaming fingers from below, grasping for me, seeking to pull me into this pit. What kind of place is this that Samuel has built? Not even built, but apparently grown underwater. And here we are flying up through the atmosphere, headed for space and Mars. My daughter captured, her crew captured or killed, Armand nowhere to be found. What exactly is my plan? How can I succeed where a whole invasion failed? There is no law or rule designating that I must succeed or survive. I've over-stepped my own power and trapped myself in this product of my lost brothers' psychological problems. I take some comfort in knowing that my genes will live on, even if my sole offspring is abused as a brood mare for interplanetary monsters. But I will not abandon my trajectory or my family. We must all experience doom. I stalk down the steps to meet mine.

A shadow exhales. I hear the soft scrape of someone's foot. I crouch and flatten myself against the inside wall. My throwing knives are burnt black so as not to reflect the light and give me away. Up and up I hear the light steps approaching. His nose appears first and I don't wait to see more. Leap from my perch, throw the knife with a perfect spin. It lands in his throat just as I catch myself against the outside wall with foot and hand, to push-off in his startled direction. He clutches the knife but I shove it in deeper. My hand covers his blood-gurgling mouth. I force him to the ground and saw that wound open until it's broader than a smile. His eyes go blank. I wipe the blade in his black uniform and leave him bleeding on the stairs.

Round and round again. How deep can this go? I find my answer at a heavy wooden door which blocks further descent. I creep up to the window, a thick pane of glass embedded at eye-level. The image is distorted. I see a naked woman bound to a bed. I see men with guns. The warped picture changes drastically with every turn of my head. Crimson curtains. Roaring fireplace. A woman bound and gagged hanging from a brick wall with hands crawling over her body. I've come to the cusp of the sex dungeon, but now what? I don't have the option of waiting for the perfect moment, or even to gather more information. How long before our castle exits the atmosphere?

I open the door. Its edges are tight and for a moment it resists, but then it swings out and I slip through the crack and let it close again behind me. Nobody's expecting me and nobody has noticed me enter. This is good, for now I can take a survey of the room.

It is indeed a dungeon. A hybrid of torture chamber and auditorium. The floor rises and falls to plateaus and pits. No proper stairs or curves, just weird wavy layers of strange-shaped brick-flooring. Plush beds rest upon some of the plateaus, each with a gorgeous naked woman strapped hand and foot, or bound with rope, ready for anybody who wanders up to her. Lone brick walls are haphazardly placed, serving no purpose but to display the enslaved beauty of the women chained to them. More than one blindfolded specimen is being whipped while suspended in the air by her leather bindings. Curtains of red, pink, black, burgundy, hang from the immensely high ceiling, perhaps hiding more sexual treasures. And of course, some of these slaves are being ravaged even as I observe them. A blonde woman is clamped in wooden stockades, bent over, as a big blond man hammers loudly into her, smacking and slapping and grunting. The whole dank room is alive with the rhythmic noises of brutally non-consensual sex acts, grunts of frustration and pleasure, wails of despair and delight. In the dancing firelight I see the silhouette of a woman, legs spread with a man pumping between them.

Samuel's men walk among this garden of

fleshly delights. Some are his security team, wearing black and weapons. Others wear t-shirts and slacks, jeans and sweaters. All grin broadly, their eyes drinking up the sexual bounty. I can see how my brother convinced so many men to join his decrepit empire. A nearly endless supply of gorgeous women brought solely for pleasure, and the glory of colonizing a new world.

It's impossible to see how far back this cavern reaches since the cascading brick walls and curtains prevent an extended view. Light shines down from glowing balls that hang from the ceiling, and fireplaces set in the walls. The crazy ceiling is a mixture of natural dripping stalactites and a chaotic network of cathedral-like masonry. Ever-flowing water fountains gush crystal clear liquid into the air before falling and collecting in pools. Along the walls I see more wooden doors, perhaps headed up to other bedrooms. I hear the muffled wailing of women wishing to be free, and the pleasured grunts of Samuel's army of rapists. How many of these are Stephanie's crew? And how many were normal women simply kidnapped off the streets? *How many can I count on to support me in a fight?*

Two men approach a woman who hangs from a wall. They're not wearing black security uniforms, just casual street-clothes. I can't see the woman's face because her head hangs down, dark curly hair hiding her breasts. The men grope her bare legs and she feebly resists, but there's nowhere for her to go.

"Jeff! Let her down!" One of the men calls out. He's looking across the room at a man on a raised platform, at a kiosk of electronic equipment, far off to my left. This man nods and presses a button, and the woman's clinking chains release her to fall into the hands of her two suitors. She screams with rage to gather her strength and tries to run, but she's weak. The men who hold her, aroused by her resistance, greedily find different ways to enjoy her lean physique. My muscles go rigid, tense with the instinct to kill them both. But I redirect my attention to where it will be most effective.

I am a bug scurrying across the floor. Invisible pest. Staying in shadow. I am the counterpart to flickering light. Leap and slither from curtain to alcove until finally I'm at the metal stairs leading up to the control kiosk. Jeff spots me. His eyes go wide and he opens his mouth to scream, hand on his pistol. But I'm already on him, dragging him down and choking him on the floor behind the panel. He can't breathe, but he can still swing his knife. So sharp it shears my beautiful beard. I grab the knife from him and stick it between his legs. The point barely pricks his undercarriage, that awful spot between ballsack and butthole, and I whisper in his ear, "You want to find out how it feels to be fucked with a knife?"

He pisses himself. I can feel the warmth emanating from his groin. And he shakes his head.

I whisper some more. "Stand up and use that control panel. Free these women. All of them."

Shaking, he stands. I stay crouched behind him, blade digging ever so lightly into his tenderest region. He stands on his tiptoes but can't escape the point. "Do it!" I hiss.

His fingers hesitate on the controls and I know he's considering something drastic and heroic. Like sounding an alarm. Somebody must have noticed a strained look on his face, or the weird way he's standing on his toes, because I hear a voice call, "Jeff! The fuck is wrong with you? You okay?"

So I wiggle the knife, and his fingers fly like magic. The sound of chimes, or tinkling of glass, echoes from every direction. It is the sound of chains and straps unloosed and it's followed by gasps of surprise and many variations of, "*What the Fuck?*"

I remove the knife from the undercarriage of my own obedient slave. Then I drag him down and free him as well, with a series of hard stabs in his worthless heart.

I stand and observe women rubbing their freed wrists, stumbling from their pedestals and beds. The men are confused, some backing away from the ladies they'd been raping. Men cluster together, many pantless, and they look up at the control panel, and see my grinning bearded face.

I open fire. They erupt in bloody wounds as the semi-automatic machine gun fire echoes off the walls.

"Women!" I scream. "I am Julius Cinnamon! *KILL THE MEN!*"

My words unleash a force of lurid destruction. The men who are slowest to act, the bewildered ones and men with their pants literally around their ankles, are the first to die. The women don't move like any combat unit. They swarm like a sea of smooth curves, sharp claws, dark eyes, and irrational rage. A man is held down, screaming as his eyes are slashed out with broken fingernails. I see an erection torn off. The clattering of chains accompanies choking sounds as men are strangled in iron. But mostly it's swarming, clawing, scratching, biting. They make short work in the chaos. Down here, for now, the women greatly outnumber the men.

I've murdered a dozen black-clad security creeps already, and the reinvigorated slave-women are taking weapons from the corpses. It's a firefight now. The retreating security men fire into the crowd of swarming pleasure-flesh, killing and maiming, but not enough to prevent the wave of wrath that spills over them. The men scream louder than the women had, as they're torn limb from limb.

I can't shoot into the crowd for fear of hurting those I came to free. And I can't reach any of my enemies before a woman finds him instead. So I just step down and walk among the glorious violence. It's true, these are indeed the most beautiful women I've ever seen. Symmetrical faces, big pretty eyes, lean waists and curvy hips. On one level I sympathize with the desire to have them ready for your pleasure at any moment. But goddamn, it's so much better to see this red-head crouch over a screaming man and sink her teeth into his throat while her friends hold him down. Blood pours over her perky little tits and she runs off with her friends to find another victim.

They come from behind the curtains and the walls. They rise up from their beds with fiery eyes. Hell hath no fury. And now they're armed and surrounding me, having dispatched all the easy meat. I can't prevent or hide my arousal. They've been abused and damaged and now they've had a taste of blood. These are my kind of women. And they keep arriving by the dozen from the curtained depths of this radical bordello.

"Stephanie!" my voice booms. "Where is my

daughter? And where is my brother?"

A woman approaches me. Her blonde hair is tied up with a bleeding string of sinew. She's stolen the boots from a dead man and stands before me with a small machine gun, a pistol, and a belt of knives strapped across her waist. There are spatters of blood across her face, her pale thighs, and smooth-shaved crotch. "I'll take you to her," she growls.

Chapter 17

They swarm like an army of murderous insects. I watch it from a balcony in Samuel's main hall. They have shown me the passageways leading from the sex dungeon to all the other rooms in this twisted castle. So anyone at any time could have easy access to a woman's warm body.

I'm crawling from the balcony up onto the long stone rafter which stretches across the ceiling of the main hall. If the outside of this replica presents a distorted version of Castle Blackburn, the inside of this main hall has multiplied the distortion into a complete deformation. The floor, far below me, is comprised of large black and white square marble tiles like a checker board. But the tiles are melted into each other, rising and falling in frozen undulation, no perfect square or flat surface to be found. The walls are the same ancient Gothic style but the perfect geometry has been stretched, bent, and shattered. Clusters of cave-rock burst through archways and push aside pillars. A dazzling stained-glass window looks out onto god-knows-what, light shining through a nonsense collection of multi-coloured chunks of glass, scattering beams of illumination to create a weird light show.

My daughter is a prisoner here. She's tied up in thick hemp rope and hanging from the ceiling, from this very rafter. Felix is bound in the same way, except that he is stark naked while she has been given the courtesy of a bearskin robe. Samuel displays his two greatest prizes and makes an example of those who would usurp him. Both are dangling in their humiliation, where they must watch the main hall that they failed to annex, and may witness the events that are happening below.

Below. A long table of black stone covered in papers and laptop computers. Set into the wall, computer terminals and large display screens. A beautiful throne of black stone and velvet cushions overlooks the hall from upon a raised platform. Samuel Saffron, Samuel Blackburn, the other son of my awful father, rests upon his throne wearing a black and white suit. He's flanked by two statues.

No, not statues. Suits of armour, like the ones who threw me out of my birth-home. The ones the dying woman warned me about.

The main hall is a bustle of activity already. A few security men and a swarm of busy workers typing on computers and scribbling on paper. They're yelling at each other, shouting orders, running in and out of the hall to do whatever tasks they've been assigned. This ship is headed for the stars, and this seems to be the centre of operations. It is into this cacophony that my ladybugs swarm.

They pour in through a dozen entrances like a deadly gas. Nude and beautiful, ebony and ivory skin and all shades in between, bearing arms. Scientists and security guards utter their surprise and are drowned out by the battle cry. The battle cry is drowned out by the sound of gunfire as the security personnel blast bloody holes in the bodies of their attackers. Women go down stumbling and bleeding, but there are more, so many more to stomp past the fallen and shoot back.

The attackers are an easier target. Samuel screeches, "Fucking Jesus! *Kill them!*" And the women fall like flies beneath a rain of bullets. I see a few retreat, the wave breaking under fear. I see my dangling daughter squirming in her bindings, muffled screams as she tries to encourage her army through the gag that makes her mute.

The floor is slippery with blood. But a surge

of renewed strength ripples through the crowd. The blond woman with the sinew in her hair stomps screaming across the floor and hurls a knife which spins like a helicopter blade slicing the air, landing in a man's face where the blade goes deep just below his eye. He goes reeling back across the room, to land in the arms of the women streaming from the opposite side. They pull the knife out of his face and begin stabbing and stabbing.

More women die and the men cluster closer and closer together at the centre of the room, up on the black stone table. But then it's too late. The unstoppable rush meets itself in the middle and rises up to completely cover the screaming men. They spare nobody. Every man aboard has been down to enjoy the dungeon, and all are complicit in the violation. The women literally tear their enemies to pieces.

The only survivors now are Samuel and a couple security men clustered around the throne. The bloodbath has subsided and the women march slowly up to the platform.

I stand on the rafter, grab the rope, and haul my daughter up from where she dangles. I lay her on the stone, pull out my knife and sever her bindings. Finally loose, she glares up at me. "You weren't supposed to come! You're butchering my men!"

I point at the bloody mess below us. "They're

not your men! They're Samuel's, and they've been raping..."

"They would have become mine!" She roars. "I want them all!"

"You were tied up and hanging from a rafter," I tell her reasonably. "*Now you're fucking free.* Take this knife and free your husband."

I gather the discarded rope and run across the rafter until I'm just above Samuel, who is cowering behind his throne. I tie it off and begin to scale down, so I can personally choke the life out of him.

The women had been swarming the platform but the two security guards have an excellent position here to spray bullets. The carnage is sickening. I thought they would have won by now, but the guards are hiding behind the suits of armour and evading counter-fire. But they're close now. Any second and the women will close in.

Someone screams, "Keep away from the suits of armour!" It's Stephanie, climbing down from the rafters onto the balcony. But her warning is too late.

These suits of armour, one carrying a long spear and the other wielding the Blackburn family sword, step forward and lift their weapons. The spear-man thrusts his weapon through one screaming mouth and out her neck, stabbing into the chest of the unlucky lady behind her. A woman kabob. A swing of my father's sword and three pretty heads go flying. Stab, thrust, slice and chop. Stomping metal monsters hack into the meat-swamp and spill blood. Bullets bounce off their chests. A few brave souls climb over the one with the spear, seeking to find a chink in his armour. He grabs one by her ankle and throws her clear across the room where her body smashes on jagged rocks and falls to the hard floor to twitch. He takes another and squeezes her screaming blond head between his two metal fists until it finally caves in. They climb over his spear and succeed in taking it from him, so he uses his metal paws to crush, break, and maim his enemies.

Meanwhile the sword continues transforming feminine beauty into dead meat. The invaders back off and try to avoid the butchery, but they've already pressed in too close and fall all over each other, unable to escape before the metal finds their tender flesh. Each suit has one surviving guard hiding behind him, taking calculated shots into the crowd.

I land beside the throne and Samuel doesn't even notice me. His eyes are glued to the violence. I could break his neck right now. I could choke him out and watch the life disappear from his eyes. But every moment these metal monsters murder another member of my mob. I leave him alone for the moment and walk with my rope to the back wall. I climb up a section of cave-like rock and hold the rope at a higher spot.

From on-high I unleash bullets into one of the security guards. His back breaks out in red spots and he collapses on the ground. I swing my aim at the second guard. My shots miss him, dinging and ringing off the hardened steel of the suit of armour. The guard breaks cover and runs before I can hit him... runs right into the open arms of the sweaty, murderous bitches who he was just slaughtering. I don't see what happens to him beneath all those arms and legs, but I hear his tortured scream cut off in a gurgling choke.

Now, holding the rope, I swing like Tarzan, feet out before me and gaining momentum. The suit of armour has a woman in his hands and is trying to rip her leg off.

My feet connect with the back of his head. He's heavier than he looks. The hard jolt of impacting metal vibrates through my skeleton and causes ripples of nausea. But he stumbles and drops the lady on the floor. He turns to grab me but I'm already swinging back. As he stumbles the women grab him and pull him down with a clattering clunk to the floor, where a crack appears across the black tile.

I land but I can't stay standing. The impact of my legs on the armour has weakened me. I stumble to the floor. And now Samuel has noticed me. He stands above me wielding a dagger. Glaring and snarling. "You've ruined everything!"

"You started it," I mutter. "Maybe we'll die here together, today."

I try to stand again, but my legs just won't stay steady. I just need a few minutes to rest. But of course I don't have it. So when Samuel falls on me with the knife, I have to grapple with him. He's much weaker than me but I don't have all my strength. The best I can do for the moment is to pin his hand on the ground, and now nobody can use his knife.

My other hand is on his throat. Tears come to my eyes. "Why is all my family sick? I escaped so I could build something great. But my own brother tore it apart and dragged me down. *Why!?*"

"You betrayed our father!" He croaks beneath my fist. "Everything you own belongs to us!"

Women go flying as the fallen suit of armour rises to his knees. One of his shoulders seems loose, crooked, but he's otherwise intact. The one with the sword is still swinging, but now the diminished crowd has backed off and he can't find a target.

A target approaches. The crowd has parted like the sea and I see Stephanie in her bearksin, hair tied back, two hands holding a massive sword. I don't know where she got it, and I'm surprised she can carry it at all. Her eyes sparkle as she approaches the suit. "This is my castle," she tells the suit. "So you're mine too. Turn around and bring me my traitorous uncle."

For a split second I entertain the hope that the monster will obey. That she could take this castle with words alone. But then the bloody sword raises up into the air. Stephanie shrugs off her bearskin and stands naked and strong before us all. Tanned skin, muscles leanly wrapped around her feminine form. The sex dungeon was full of gorgeous women, but none of them approach the fierce beauty of my stunning daughter as she faces down whatever this thing is whose sword is plummeting like a meteor toward her brazen face. She swings her weapon like a baseball bat to meet the oncoming blade. An ear-busting ring and a spark of light. Stephanie goes reeling back, but she still holds her weapon. The suit vibrates visibly, so much that he's blurry. Stephanie takes another swing, aiming for his head, but he blocks it with his other hand. He forms a fist around the blade and she can't pull it free. He suddenly jerks the sword back and she tumbles toward him. He jabs his own sword out at her belly, and she barely jumps aside. Still, he nicks the skin of her belly and the blood pours down onto her thick brown muff.

Now he has two swords and she has none.

Yet she grins, feet apart, ready to pounce, a fool like her father.

A wall explodes. Stone and rock fly across the room, crushing equipment. A tall figure walks through the dust from the darkness of the room beyond. Before I can discern his face I hear Armand's French accent say, "Step back, Miss Cinnamon."

He tosses a grenade at the suit of armour even as Stephanie lunges behind a chunk of fallen stone. The suit swings its sword and connects with the grenade, which explodes on impact. The suit stumbles backwards, almost loses the grip of his weapon. But then he throws the Blackburn family broadsword like a throwing knife, spinning and spinning through the air toward Armand. Armand has pulled the pin on another grenade and has hauled his arm back to lob the explosive. The sword-throw is either perfectly aimed or perfectly lucky, for the blade slices through his shoulder. The grenade and the hand are now separate from the body, unable to throw. I see it all in stark clarity, in slow motion, the grenade with pin pulled beginning to fall as blood escapes the severed shoulder, and that evil sword spins undaunted by its devastating victory. I wonder, in this frozen moment, does Armand have time to escape before the explosion kills him? Can he jump out of the way?

I see his lean body moving. But is he leaping to safety? No. His other hand flashes behind him and grabs the hilt of the sword in mid-spin before his severed hand even hits the ground. His whole body shakes visibly as his skeleton absorbs the momentum of the projectile. Then his body becomes a catapult. An unleashed spring. He throws the sword overhand and sends it spinning back at the metal monster. Just as the handle leaves his fingertips his grenade explodes at his feet. Armand, my most trusted ally, is splattered upon the nearby floor and walls. Grotesquely, his head remains whole and flies through the air still wearing shades and a grin that seems to say, "Goodbye, Mr. Cinnamon." The energy of the explosion adds inhuman force to the flying blade which whirs like a spinning bullet through the air. The blade cleaves the helmet of the suit of armour. Splits it right in two, stuck deep in the middle. The spin of the blade is so severe that the metal suit somersaults backwards once before landing on its back, slamming onto the marble floor with shattering force. Black and white chunks fly up into the air. Sparks of electricity shoot from its broken face and I spy the wires and circuitry inside. Stephanie has already leaped on the fallen robot and is wrenching the weapon out.

Naked Felix and the naked women have tied ropes around the limbs of the other suit, working together to try to pull him apart. Felix is like a Greek god, his muscles rippling as he hauls on the strained cord. The enemy's metal body is stretched out, but they don't have the strength to dismantle him. Stephanie approaches with her sword, the family sword which she seems to have inherited, and she begins hacking at his neck. Wedges the tip between two metal plates. Drives it deeper as sparks erupt.

In my shock, watching Armand die, I allowed Samuel to slip from my grasp. He's running now. Running to an exit. I abandon the crowd, leaving my daughter to claim the castle and victory, and I chase my brother. So I can prevent him from whatever ugliness he might do next. So I can look into his eyes and see if there's any flicker of true brotherhood. Is he a mere copy of my cruel father? Or has he been twisted into a monster by my father's cruelty?

Round and round we go, down more spiralling stairs. I hear his breath and the patter of his feet. We orbit the central pole like electrons orbiting the path of a nucleus. I call out, "Brother! Stop this. You're defeated and the castle belongs to Stephanie. But you don't have to die. You're young and there's room for you in this universe. I want to know my brother! If I knew you existed I would have stolen you away and taught you the things that nobody taught me!"

The descending shadow does not speak but instead grunts in strained frustration and runs even faster from me. I hear the hissing sound of a sealed door opening and I reach the bottom before it closes again.

I burst through the door. It takes a moment to appreciate what I'm looking at. This is a vast room, perhaps comprising the entire bottom floor of the castle. The ceiling is high and the floor deep, but this door has let me onto a raised stone walkway that goes all along the outer walls. Below me, spread out across the whole expanse, is a series of rivers.

It is these rivers that first confuse my senses. Each one flows in a perfect circle upon the stone floor, with no bank to hold it in. There are seven in total, in concentric circles, and each river flows in the opposite direction from its neighbours. Each flows eternally into itself, a liquid snake eating its own tail. Inspecting closer I see that these rivers do not even touch the stone tiles of the floor. Some invisible force keeps the liquid raised and formed into a rushing tube with waves warbling on the surface but never a drop splashed or spilled. And they glow, each circle a different colour, casting wavy lights on the thick pillars supporting the high ceiling.

At the very centre is a hole in the floor. From so far back I cannot see what lies in that hole, but a dim blue light shines up and I imagine that one could look down that orifice and behold the distant Earth below. Frighteningly I imagine all these liquids losing their majestic shapes and pouring down that drain. I never learned how the so-called "anti-magnet drive" works, but I form the impression that I'm seeing it in action right now.

The stone balcony encloses the room's perimeter, but a grid of metal catwalks criss-crosses its area. Samuel's boots clang loudly with echoing footstomps across that metal mesh. I pursue. He's headed for the centre, where the catwalk forms a ring around the hole. He has a good head start and reaches the computer terminal. His hands fly, pressing buttons. Then he pulls on one of several large levers. Below me I see the waves of the rivers deepen in their undulating flow. A yellow blob separates from its source and drips inwards toward the blue stream. When yellow hits blue the whole blue circle loses its shape and becomes a crazy wobbling mess. The floor shakes. I'm thrown into the air and grab the railing to keep from falling down into the blue liquid below. Do I hear rocks crumbling? Metal wrenching? The yellow drop has separated into erratic beads that harass the blue river, which seems to somehow try to correct its path. They want to go in their neat circles, but Samuel is somehow disrupting them.

On shaky feet I gain the rumbling catwalk again and throw a series of knives at my distant brother. But my aim cannot be true in this shaking and quaking room. The knives go wide, nowhere close to target, and I dare not try my pistol among such important equipment.

I can't relate with his pettiness. I've done brutal things in the name of a worthy cause, or sometimes just to relish my own sweet power, but Samuel has come down her to unwind his own hard work just to spite his own family. I grip the shaking railing and observe him, trying to understand how a mind can become so twisted.

Now it's a struggle to move forward. Can I reach him before he scatters these orderly fluids? One step at a time, holding the rail. "Samuel!" I scream. "I never caused your pain! I took nothing from you! Why do you hate me?"

He's working heavily to push and pull great levers out of alignment. He puts his back in it, shaking, breaking a sweat, and the rivers below shake and wobble with increasing disorder. As he pushes one lever, the others gravitate back to their original positions. If I can get him away from the panel the whole system may correct itself.

He looks at me with crazy eyes, snarling. The casual and sarcastic humour that I saw when I first met him, before I knew who he truly was as he sat at the desk at Jasserty Salvage, is gone. "Because I didn't want to be your replacement!" he screams at me. "He would have left me with my mom, like all his other bastards. But you had to run away, so he needed a replacement... and I could never escape! Well neither can you! And if I have to be your replacement... everything that's yours belongs to me! You won't take it all again!"

Mad emotion fuels his efforts and he pushes a lever further and further, so the whole world tilts. I wonder what's happening on the floors above. Green liquid swirls and spirals toward the centre, and then is pulled with horrendous speed out the hole.

I reach him. Grab his shoulder and pull him back. He responds with a knife and gets it deep in my shoulder. We collapse together and behind him the lever moves slowly back toward its original position. He's twisting the knife so I kick him away. He stumbles back at the panels, slams into a lever, and a great pink blob raises shining up into the air from below. It lands on a section of catwalk, crushing the metal and scattering the liquid. The whole network of walkways shifts and bends. The whole castle is an earthquake in the sky. Samuel is screaming with rage, tears streaming down his eyes as he pushes on the stick. I hear a deep cracking noise and see light pouring up from cracks in the floor. More precious liquid escapes. He'll kill us all.

Now we're tilted downwards. Now I'm leaping at my lost sibling. Now my weight slams into him and carries us over the panel and over the railing. Now we're falling together, down the drain, down the centre hole.

Suddenly I can see the castle from below, shrinking into the darkening blue sky. Those swirling balls spin around it like electrons. I'm falling through the empty air.

I realize that I'm going to die.

Deep breath of the thin atmosphere.

The clarity of the world, communicated through my senses, is exquisite. The cosmic mystery is speaking to me directly via this vast blue panorama. I hope I've listened closely, my love, all my life.

I'm still holding onto my brother. Now I grip his shoulders as the air rushes past us, making a mess of clothes and hair. I grip him hard. I look into his wide-open eyes. I yell so he can hear me over the wind. "I already built Agartha, and she will thrive without me! Stephanie will colonize Mars with your equipment and the women and scientists you kidnapped! We both die today, but the human race will be transformed. We set it in motion, and now we hand it off. You did this. *We did this!*"

His hands are on my elbows, squeezing. He clamps his eyes tightly closed. His tears are blown away by the wind. I hug him with all my strength, and I feel him squeeze back. My only brother. The only one who understands where I came from, and what ugliness can do to the human heart. Somehow I love him, and I believe that now I've shown him that. So I push him away. Because the ground is rushing up to meet us, and we must all meet our doom alone.

My final thoughts are my own. No need to share them here.

Chapter 18

Climb, bitch, climb!

Daddy looms over me in the busy sky, staring up at the red unknown rather than down at his daughter, shaming me for being so slow. Hand over fist I hurl myself up the rock wall, grabbing outcropping and crevice. Blood pumps through my muscles. They're eager for exhaustion. In the Martian gravity I can throw myself higher than I could on Earth, leaping with my bare hands toward the towering peak so far above.

We made sure his statue was taller than the castle, and forged from Martian metal. But now Castle Blackburn flies again and will soon tower over him. Those crooked spires cut the light out of the dusty sky for a hundred years. Now they aim to go home to space-darkness. Unless I can invade her again.

Our valley is ringed with these spiky mountains. We landed the castle on one peak, where a natural path leads down to the bottom. The dark fortress could be seen from any vantage point below. We built his statue on an opposing peak. A barrel-chested and bearded beast in a suit, raging up at the sky with a scream on his lips and a starward sparkle in his eye, breaking the chains on his wrists like King Kong. On the other peaks we built the rocket ramps, launch pads, radio towers, satellite dishes, and wind turbines.

On this lonely peak we built nothing. Until now. Now I'm building a makeshift stairway, not by shaping the Earth but by seeing each imperfection in the rock wall as a pre-existing step in a desperate staircase. Also, my unmanageable, castle-stealing sons are building a shadow on this peak as Castle Blackburn passes between myself and the Sun. I can't spot good handholds in this temporary darkness, but I can't spare a moment to slow down. So I leap again at a shadow which appears to be a little ledge. But it's not a ledge and I slip, fall, scrambling hand and foot over the smooth sheer drop. Deadly distance awaits below. Shall I meet the same fate as my father?

My left hand catches something. A little ledge, barely big enough for two fingers. Enormous strain on those little digits, but my descent desists. Dangling, I look from the blackness of the castle down to the valley below. What my sons are leaving behind. What could have been theirs. What took a century to build.

The fields of fungus and cinnamon trees, genetically engineered to thrive in this hostile environment and generate oxygen, offering food tastier than the endless supply of nano-fabricated dirt-bars for our scientists and engineers.

Keep climbing! My shoulder muscles surge beneath my suit. My breath pants inside my helmet. The castle is approaching the peak. I need to be there to grab the stones, to pull myself in, to unseat my treacherous offspring and take back the castle I earned so long ago. To show them that their future is not flying through space but building on what we've started here.

They're leaving behind the shining steel rows of rock-eater factories. Yrja and Agartha mass-produced the nanobots after they got the key to Daddy's safe deposit box from his splattered corpse. Now we put in rocks and get out almost any material we want. From the disgusting-but-nutritious dirt-bars to more nanobots.

They're leaving behind the pleasure-dome where twelve of my thirteen children were conceived. A steaming sauna of a garden greenhouse, the home of our society's ultra-social mating ritual. You go in to hunt for a mate, or to be hunted. I go there a lot, and anybody may fuck their Ice Queen if they can catch her. But so far only Felix has ever had the strength to hold me down and give me babies.

The shadow slides up the hill faster than I can. There's still a chance I can make it. I scream and grunt, send rocks tumbling.

They're leaving behind their mother.

They're leaving behind our alliance with

Agartha, who shared with us their anti-ageing drugs and new ways to generate electricity, as we shared with them our cloning and neuro-synthesis inventions. Daddy left me nothing in his will, because almost everything he owned had been in my name the whole time, and nobody knew except him. Uncle Sammy had wanted him to sign it all over, but he'd already made sure that only I had the legal power to give away Agartha. So when I found out that it was all mine, I signed it over to Yrja. Mars is mine. Earth is hers.

The base of the castle slams into the very peak, cracking it and sending pieces over the other side. I have to hold on tight for a shaking moment, and then continue my ascent. I reach the shattered tip and leap. Back arching, legs like springs, I feel every inch of my lithe frame grasping and stretching. But it's not enough. My fingers brush the rocky bottom, just barely, and I fall through the air over the other side.

It's not as long a fall on this side, and not as steep. I've climbed up out of the valley chasing my renegade home and now I'm tumbling down a grainy hill toward the fields of solar-panels beyond. I land on my back, defeated.

The castle shrinks into the sky among the flying saucers and the steady, automated stream of seed-rockets which we launch into space to auto-terraform distant planets. My sword is on that ship. And a lock cut from my father's beard.

I'm disappointed at my failure, but as I watch them escape I smile with pride at the success of my babies. Of course they want to leave. There's nothing for them to hunt here. When we first arrived the harshness of Mars' environment was a sufficient enemy and we battled it like a monster. But that was before most of my sons were born and they're greedy for their own adventure. It's safe here. Our colony is a success. So I need to frequent the pleasure-dome to find a physical challenge, to be part of a hunt, to unleash my animal.

We're not Martians just like we're not Earthlings. We're travellers, conquerors, adventurers. So they left me behind like I tried to leave Daddy behind.

I climb back up the peak so I can get a good look at the escapees. A hot air balloon appears from the other side, and riding in its basket is a friendly face. My rugged Felix with his beard and scars, come to save me.

"We can still catch them!" He booms as I leap onto the basket. He helps to pull me in. "The fools know how slow it rises, how long it takes to accelerate. Our balloon can get on top of them before they leave the atmosphere!"

Castle Blackburn passes just beneath Phobos, and for a few perfect moments the small and irregular shape of the little moon is captured between those black spires. I think of Greek gods castrating their fathers and eating their children.

I shake my head. "No."

The castle passes on but my eyes remain fixed on the little moon. I imagine Phobos transformed. I imagine it covered in its own castle-spires, these ones sparkling crystal for its Ice Queen. The whole moon a great travelling fortress. I imagine it hollowed out with an anti-magnet drive, or some other means of propulsion, running through its centre.

My mind wanders further. Mass producing monsters, and heroes to battle them. With the anti-ageing drugs I can give birth to endless generations of hunters and adventurers. Travel the stars in my sparkling ice castle. Spreading our inventions, our genes, and our insatiable will. Let my sons have their castle. Their lack of imagination disappoints me. My new palace will be bigger and faster, radiant like a star.

My children are free, independent, and beyond my control. My next ambition occupies all of my being in this moment of perfect revelation. To leave this place behind to the workers, as I did with Earth. To gather all our learning and inventions once more into a shining seed and go impregnate the cosmos. I want to see other suns, multiple star systems, black holes, neutron stars. I want to live a million years and nurture a billion new forms of life, propel them all into the unknown on the winds of a mothers' love. And if there's anybody out there to hunt, any alliances to form, or any mesmerizing abyss to fall into, I want to be there. Maybe some day I'll find a planet with somebody strong enough to kill me.

But today I go with Felix down to the pleasure-dome where we run naked through the misty forest. It's alive with the sound of love. Panting and slapping. Playful women are thrown down and gloriously ravaged. I evade the lean nerds who seek to conquer their queen. I allow one man to grab me, throw me down, and climb upon me as I pretend to be overpowered. I let him kiss me and spread my legs, just so Felix can grab him and throw him off. Felix's sparkling eyes and hairy chest tower over me. Then my Russian bear proceeds to truly conquer me. I don't have to allow him. I resist him, because only by resisting can I be overcome by my only worthy lover. I lay on my back in the bushes, looking over his shoulder up through the curved glass of the pleasure-dome where Julius Cinnamon's metal likeness looms like a god. The shadows of the lines in his hard face are so perfect. I reach out impossibly to him. His face is turned up, searching the sky, and I reach beyond him to Phobos which will soon be mine. Felix wraps his hand in my hair and buries his face in the smooth skin of my neck. As I feel him enter me I whisper in his ear, for the thousandth time, *"Daddy."*

ABOUT THE AUTHOR

Matt Payne was born in Corner Brook, Newfoundland. He worked as a line-cook and factory worker in New Brunswick, Quebec, and Ontario. He studied journalism at St. Thomas University in Fredericton. Matt is an author, electronic musician, audio producer, wretched dork, and serious businessman. He lives in Ottawa.

Other books by Matt Payne:

Robot God / Hybrid Brain

The Paranoid Adventures of Larry Grank

The Sick Book of Lies

Neo-Something Doom Puzzle

Dinosaur Mountain

www.pattmayne.com
www.spiralmachines.ca